KARTER

Dark Secrets of the Gilded Elite

Author OLIVIA COLDWELL

Disclaimer:

Blue Wild Horse LLC
5830 E 2ND ST, STE 7000 #18169
CASPER, WY 82609

Website: www.bluewildhorse.com

Book Cover by BWH

Illustrations by BWH

[01] edition 2024 ISBN: 979-8-218-49780-4
"Karter: Dark Secrets of the Gilded Elite"

This book is 346 pages long.

In the opulent enclave of Greenwood Hills, where power and prestige define the social order, appearances are often dangerously deceptive. Alex Karter, heir to a vast financial empire, finds his world unraveling when his father, Richard Karter, becomes the prime suspect in a shocking murder investigation. As deeply buried secrets from decades of wealth and privilege begin to emerge, Alex and his journalist friend Lucas find themselves drawn into a labyrinthine investigation fraught with lies, betrayal, and deadly corruption.

Set against the backdrop of grand estates and glittering high-society gatherings, "Karter: Dark Secrets of the Gilded Elite" transports readers into a world where every whispered conversation could hide a dark conspiracy, and where Alex's relentless pursuit of the truth threatens to dismantle his family's carefully constructed legacy. Amidst the elegance and excess, he must navigate treacherous secrets that could bring everything crashing down.

This gripping family saga expertly balances fast-paced action with deep, introspective moments, peeling back layers of mystery with every chapter. The richly detailed settings and immersive atmosphere pull readers into the heart of high society, where every detail, from the rustle of designer gowns to the whispers behind closed doors, heightens the tension and intrigue.

"Karter: Dark Secrets of the Gilded Elite" is a riveting tale of betrayal, corruption, and suspense, where every revelation exposes an additional threat. Immerse in captivating narrative, uncover world where each secret topples powerful.

TABLE OF CONTENT

CHAPTER 1

THE CHARITY GALA

In Greenwood Hills, people not only expected perfection but also meticulously designed it in their illusions. In Greenwood Hills, illusions reign as people design perfection. Large mansions lined the cobbled streets, their immaculate lawns testified to the silent competition of the elite. Every day, you could see the socialites exchanging pleasantries, their conversations as polite as the facades of their houses.

Alex Karter maneuvered this world, despite feeling like an outsider. Her life was a delicate balance between fitting in and preserving her individuality. As a financial analyst, he often found himself at the center of the city's network of influence, but his analytical mind kept him abreast of the undercurrents that others seemed to ignore. This morning, the city was buzzing with anticipation for the annual charity gala. The event, held at the prestigious Country Club, was the highlight of the social calendar. Alex expected an opulent evening, a veneer concealing brewing tensions.

Alex's morning routine was a ritual of calm before the social storm. He stood by the window, looking out over the manicured gardens of the Karter Estate, the morning sun casting long shadows on the dewy grass. The rich aroma of ground coffee filled the spacious kitchen, an aroma that always brought her a sense of peace.

He poured himself a cup, savoring the warmth that spread in his hands. As he took his first sip, the familiar sound of his mother's footsteps echoed down the hall. Margaret Karter entered, her presence as graceful as ever. Dressed in a tailored suit, her silver hair coiffed, she embodied the elegance that the city demanded.

"Hello, Alex," she said, her voice warm but tinged with the usual shade of concern.

"Hello, mom," Alex replied, putting down his cup. "Big day ahead."

Margaret nodded, her eyes meeting his with a mixture of pride and concern. "Indeed. The gala is always an important event. Your father has high hopes for tonight."

Alex smiled, the corners of his mouth lifting. "He always does."

Margaret came closer, her hand resting on his shoulder. "Just be yourself, Alex. That's all we're asking for."

Alex's gaze went to the window, his thoughts a whirlwind of anticipation and discomfort. "Sometimes I wonder if being myself is enough."

Margaret's grip tightened, a gesture of both comfort and firmness. "It is, Alex. More than enough."

He turned to her, searching her eyes for reassurance. "I just don't want to disappoint him. Or you."

"You could never disappoint us," Margaret said, her expression softening. Remember, tonight is more than just the gala. It's about showing who you are and what you stand for."

Alex nodded, the weight of his words sinking in. I'll try to remember that.

Margaret smiled, a rare, sincere smile that made her look years younger. "That's all I ask."

As the morning light bathed the kitchen in a golden hue, Alex felt a surge of determination. He finished his coffee and put the cup down with a decisive clatter. "I should get ready. A lot needs to be done before tonight.

Margaret stepped back a step, giving him a nod of approval. "I'll see you later. And Alex,"she paused, her voice soft but firm, "trust your instincts. They never led you astray."

He watched her leave, her words lingering in the air like a whispered promise. Alex took a deep breath and faced the day, prepared to navigate Greenwood Hills' social dance. Tonight would be a test of his resilience, his patience, and his unyielding quest for the truth. Regardless of the gala's secrets, he was determined to take up the challenge.

The Karter Mansion, a testament to the family's wealth and status, was a mixture of classic elegance and modern sophistication. Margaret decorated each room, reflecting her impeccable taste. Alex felt burdened by the story and expectations as he walked through the halls.

Portraits of ancestors with stern faces adorned the long corridors, their eyes seeming to follow Alex as he moved. The mansion's grandeur intimidated even those who grew up there. A family that prioritized tradition and prestige above all else was clear through the intricate moldings, antique furniture, and soft, ambient lighting.

Richard Karter's study was in stark contrast to the rest of the house. The dark wood paneling and the leather-bound books gave it a solemn, almost oppressive atmosphere. The smell of aged paper and polished wood filled the room, creating a sanctuary where Richard directed the family's affairs with unwavering concentration.

Richard looked up from his desk as Alex walked in. His father was a tall man, his presence imposing and authoritarian. He always dressed, with his tie tied and his suit tailored to perfection.

"Alex, are you ready for tonight?"Richard's voice carried the weight of authority, his piercing gaze fixed on his son.

"Almost, dad," Alex replied, standing in the doorway. He admired his father's ability to arouse respect, but he often found the weight of expectations overwhelming. A thick atmosphere of unspoken pressure filled the room.

Tori, the daughter of Eleonor Blackwood laughed "Me? I'm just trying to navigate through it all without losing my mind."

Their conversation interrupted when the first course, a presented a plate of seared scallops with a delicate citrus sauce, arrived.

Since the father took over the business, the household staff has gained experience in organizing social events for the Karter family.

While they were eating, Alex couldn't help but observe the surrounding interactions. He noted the subtle glances and calm exchanges between the guests, each one being a piece of the complex social puzzle that defined this city. Lucas, still a journalist, was engaged in a lively discussion with the person next to him, his eyes riveted with curiosity.

Tori, a young 30-year-old lawyer, sensing Alex's distraction, dabbed his arm. "You're always watching, aren't you?"

Alex smiled. "It's a habit that I can't seem to break."

Tori nodded. "That's right. And sometimes the most interesting stories are the ones that are not told."Approached their table with a radiant smile, his presence attracting attention.

Are you enjoying this good time Alex? she said

"That's wonderful, Mrs. Blackwood," Alex replied, raising his glass to toast. "You have surpassed yourself."

"Thank you, Alex," Eleanor said, her gaze scanning the table. "I am so glad that you were all able to join us. Tonight, it's not just about raising money; it's about celebrating our community and the bonds that unite us."

The conversation shifted to lighter topics as the dinner progressed, with classes flowing from one to the other. Alex enjoyed Tori's company, her wit and her insight, a refreshing change from the often superficial chatter of such events.

As dessert was served a decadent chocolate mousse topped with gold leaf-Tori turned to Alex with a more serious expression. "There's something I wanted to ask you."

Alex put down his spoon, his curiosity piqued. "What is it?"

Tori hesitated for a moment, her eyes searching his. Do you know the reason behind Daniel Thornton's return to town?"

Alex pondered her question. "I have heard some rumors, but nothing concrete. Why do you ask?"

Tori glanced around to make sure they weren't being overheard. Something about him doesn't suit me. He's always been unpredictable, even in our youth. I just felt that his return will shake things up. That's his investigative side."

Alex nodded, understanding his concern. "I had the same feeling. There is more to his story."

Tori smiled; her serious attitude lifted. "Shall we dance?"

Alex stood up and held out his hand. "It would be with pleasure."

As they made their way to the dance floor, the festivities of the evening continued around them. Alex, however, found true intrigue in undiscovered secrets and mysteries.

Richard stood up, adjusting his tie as he spoke. "Tonight's event is crucial. We have important connections to make. Remember, it's not just about us. This is the family heirloom."

"I know, dad," Alex replied, trying to match his father's serious demeanor. He felt a powerful message from his father, who revived his strong bond with the responsibilities of family affairs while protecting himself from a hostile environment in the heart of a city itself loaded with competitors and less and less recommendable people.

Richard walked over to a cupboard and poured himself a glass of whisky, the ice tinkling as he turned the glass. "We have built a reputation over the generations. It's your responsibility to enforce that, Alex. Tonight, more than ever, we must show our strength and our unity. "

Alex nodded, swallowing hard. "I understand. I'll do my best."

Richard pointing his finger from his hand that lifts his glass "not your best Alex, you will show them your strength, and that the KARTER family is not extinct no matter what" of a deep paternal affirmation but also of the harsh patriarch forged by previous affairs.

While they were talking, the door opened and Margaret entered. Her figure highlighted her couture dress, which gave her another rather attractive age. His presence always brought a sense of calm into the room, a gentle contrast to Richard's severity. She moved with the grace of someone who mastered the art of social diplomacy.

"Margaret, you look gorgeous," Richard said, his tone softening as he looked at his wife. There was a rare warmth in his eyes when he addressed her like a young man desiring his young mistress.

"Thank you, Richard," she replied, smiling. Her gaze turned to Alex, her eyes filled with pride and encouragement. "And Alex, you seem quite dashing yourself."

"Thanks, Mom," Alex said, feeling a little more comfortable. Margaret's approval always calmed her nerves, even if it was only a little. Her soothing smile relieved the day's tension.

Margaret approached Alex, adjusting her bow tie with a trained hand. "You will be wonderful tonight, Alex. Remember to stay true to yourself."

Richard watched the interaction, a slight smile on his lips. "Listen to your mother, Alex. She always knows best, and if she adds your bow tie, it's because she wants to have the last word on what I just told you."

Alex took a deep breath, feeling a surge of determination. "I will remember that."

Margaret's eyes shone with affection. Remember to enjoy yourself, even if it's. It's a party, after all."

Alex nodded, the knot of anxiety loosening. "I'll try, mom."

The three of them stood in the study, the room held its breath. Tonight is crucial for the KARTER family, and Alex understood his actions' long-lasting impact on this magnificent mansion.

With a last nod, Richard raised his glass. "To the legacy of Karter."

"To KARTER's legacy," Alex and Margaret echoed, their voices melting into a silent affirmation of the bond that united them.

The evening ahead would test Alex in unimaginable ways, but for now, with his family's support, he felt hopeful and ready to face the challenge.

Driving to the Country Club meant taking the city's most scenic roads. Autumn leaves painted the landscape in shades of gold and red, a striking contrast to the pristine lawns and well-groomed hedges that lined the streets. The black luxury car of the KARTER family glided along the road, the hum of the engine serving as a soft backdrop for the conversation inside.

Margaret was sitting in the backseat next to Alex, her elegance undiminished by the confined space of the car. Richard, in the passenger seat, glanced back. He behaved, like a seasoned wise man. His athletic build elevated the driver, a stoic figure in an impeccable uniform, walked the familiar road with ease.

Leaving Carter Mansion, the car brimmed with anticipation. Margaret's gentle reminders about etiquette and Richard's briefings on potential business allies filled the car ride, their voices weaving together in a transparent tapestry of expectations.

"Remember, Alex, the Thompsons will be here tonight. It is crucial that we get their support for the upcoming project," said Richard, in an unshakable tone.

Alex nodded; his gaze fixed on the passing landscape. "I know, Dad. I've been reading about their recent ventures."

"Good," Richard replied, a hint of approval in his voice. "They are essential for our next step. A strong relationship with them could open many doors."

Margaret, still a diplomat, leaned in, her voice soft but firm. "And don't forget to congratulate Mrs. Thompson on her new art collection. She is very proud of it. It would mean a lot to her."

Alex's mind drifted to the other side of his life, where he could be himself, not the KARTER legacy heir. "Understood, mom. Compliment the art collection," he said.

The car entered a panoramic road, the outdoor landscape turned into a vivid demonstration of autumnal splendor. The vibrant reds, oranges and yellows of the leaves created a fascinating contrast with the deep green of the conifers, the sky when it does not appease this heavy atmosphere, the thick clouds darkened the horizon. Alex found comfort in the beautiful surroundings, a temporary escape from impending pressures.

Margaret, catching his far-off gaze, placed a steadying hand on his knee. "Alex, I get this event feels like a burden, you independent man. But remember, it's the family's support that will help you shine as you should."

Alex reached out and touched her hand, offering reassurance.

Richard clears his throat, getting Alex's attention again. "Also, monitor Daniel Thornton. He's been out of town for years, but his return could mean he had plans. We need to evaluate his intentions., and trying to find out from our guests new information about Daniel"

"Daniel Thornton," Alex repeated, sorting out the name. "I'll keep that in mind."

As the large doors opened, the car approached the entrance to the Country Club. The groundskeepers maintain the club, as evidenced by the rolling lawns and trimmed hedges, which testify to its prestige. The building itself was a monument to the wealth of the city, its architecture a mixture of classical elegance and modern sophistication.

As they neared the main entrance, exciting the activity became clear. Valets in sharp uniforms moved, guiding guests and parking cars with proven ease. The soft glow of the lanterns illuminated the path, casting a warm and inviting light.

Margaret took a deep breath, smoothing the fabric of her dress. Alex, if only my dress could disappear like the memories. »

Alex started laughing, which made him relax his jaw. "You always kept your sense of derision, mom"

Car stopped, driver quickly got out to open door. Richard came out first, reaching out to help Margaret. Alex followed, adjusting his suit jacket as he walked down the gravel road. The evening air was fresh, carrying the light scent of pine and autumn leaves.

The evenings bring a refreshing chill that soothes the soul.

Alex takes up his mother's scarf out of kindness.

Richard giving Alex one last look at his entire outfit. "You remind me of when I was your age. I had this posture that I held from my grandfather., a hell of a character!"

Margaret smiled; "I confirm, you looked great.. you have kept the charisma".

Margaret, Richard, and Alex climbed the steps, joining the elite crowd. The guests were a real who's who of the city's social scene, each one more elegantly dressed than the previous one. The women's dresses glittered in the light, showcasing the marks of large quilts, while the men dressed in tailored suits and tuxedos.

Despite the varying ages, the identical sizes suggested the guests were from the KARTER family.

They scattered paintings of famous artists at the entrances and arranged bouquets the size of a young adult at equal intervals to guide the guests to the place of convergence.

"Margaret, Richard, Alex!"a familiar voice shouted. It was Eleanor Blackwood, the host of the evening. Her very light dress, making her forget the season and gave her a charm to her figure.

"Eleanor," Richard greeted her with a charming smile, stepping forward to kiss her on the cheek. "You have surpassed yourself, as always." She holds her hands to him with her outstretched arms with an air of admiration for the mature man that Richard embodied.

Margaret returned Eleanor's compliment with a graceful nod. "You are too kind, Eleanor. This evening is magnificent."

Alex offered a polite smile, feeling the weight of Eleanor's sharp and calculating gaze. "I'm all right, thank you, Mrs. Blackwood. It's a pleasure to see you again."

Eleanor's eyes, always attentive, seemed to evaluate Alex for a moment before she smiled warmly. "You have become quite your father's young man, Alex. I recall you as a young boy, running around, searching for the finest champagne.

Alex chuckled, even if the memory brought him a twinge of nostalgia. "Time flies by, doesn't it, and for champagne I keep the good habits?"

"Indeed it is," Eleanor nodded. She turned her attention to Richard and Margaret. "I hope you enjoy the evening. We have a whole range of entertainment, and of course, the auction promises to be exciting."

Richard nodded. I have complete faith in your ability to make this evening as successful as the previous ones.

Eleanor's smile widened, her eyes sparkling with a mixture of pride and mystery. "I hope so. Now, if you'll excuse me, I have to take care of other guests. Please, make yourself at home."

As Eleanor moved through the crowd, greeting and charming the other guests, Alex couldn't help but admire her ability to command the room. Despite the whispers and rumors that often surrounded her, Eleanor Blackwood remained an unshakable pillar of the social scene.

Richard put a reassuring hand on Alex's shoulder. "Stay close, and we will sail together."

As he moved around the room, he spotted Lucas Bennett, his best friend, standing near the edge of the crowd. Lucas, in a sharp suit, nursed champagne and scanned the room like a shrewd journalist. Alex walked over to him, relieved to see a friendly face amid the sea of formalities.

"Lucas, good to see you," Alex greeted him, happy. He held out his hand, which Lucas shook.

"Alex, likewise," Lucas replied with a smile. "Ready for another new evening?"

Alex replied in a direct tone, the tension in his shoulders easing. "You know that. By the way, did you see anything interesting?"

Lucas's eyes shone with the thrill of a new story. He leaned closer, his voice lowering to a conspiratorial whisper. "yes. There's a new face in town, someone who's making a splash."

Alex raised an eyebrow, intrigued. "Oh? Who's that?"

Lucas glanced around, making sure they weren't being heard. "Daniel Thornton. After years of absence, he appeared tonight with a clear agenda. People are talking."

Alex felt a surge of curiosity. "Daniel Thornton, this name rings a bell. What's his plan?"

Lucas shrugged his shoulders, a mischievous gleam in his eyes. "That's what I'm trying to find out. However, his return seems to unsettle many.

While they were talking, a server passed by, offering a tray of champagne. Alex took a drink, the fresh stem a reassuring weight in his hand. "Well, I guess tonight has become a little more interesting."

"Indeed," Lucas nodded, taking a sip from his drink. Stay vigilant, Alex. There's always more going on here than it seems."

Alex nodded, scanning the room with renewed concentration. "It always is. Let me know if you dig up anything else."

Lucas smiled. "Will do. Have some fun, even if just a little."

Alex smiles, feeling a rare moment of camaraderie amid the superficiality of the gala. "I'll try. Thank you, Lucas."

As Lucas blended into the crowd, Alex's thoughts turned to Daniel Thornton. The evening had taken on an additional layer of intrigue, and he could not shake the feeling that whatever Thornton's return meant, he was bound to stir up the carefully maintained tranquility.

The music of the orchestra swelled, filling the ballroom with a rich, melodic sound. Alex moved through the crowd with a renewed sense of purpose, exchanging pleasantries and mentally taking notes on the conversations. He felt the weight of the evening weighing down on him, the unspoken expectations of his family and the hidden currents of the social elite.

Alex sensed the hidden story beneath the glamour. Tonight, his determination was to uncover the truth, unveil the hidden reality.

While mingling, he caught intriguing snippets of conversation about Thornton. A puzzle from the past reappeared, tempting Alex's analytical mind.

With one last deep breath, he navigated the twists and turns of the evening, ready to dive into the mysteries that awaited him. The grand ballroom, with all its splendor, was just the beginning.

Alex joined Luca again. The latter nodded towards a tall, athletic man standing near the entrance. "Daniel Thornton. A distant relative of the Blackwoods, apparently. He's been gone for years."

Alex followed Lucas's gaze, seizing the imposing presence of the stranger. Daniel's black hair and piercing green eyes seemed to sweep the room with a mixture of curiosity and calculation. His elegant but discreet outfit distinguished him from the flamboyant displays around him.

"Interesting," Alex whispered. "He stands out."

"Isn't it?" Lucas said, his journalistic instincts on high alert. "I heard whispers about him. It looks like he has a history with the Blackwood family."

Alex nodded. "A story, eh? I wonder what kind of story."

Lucas leaned over, lowering his voice. "he left under less than favorable circumstances. Rumor has it that there was an argument involving Eleanor, but the details remain unknown.

Eleanor became involved in the exchange that had begun between Alex and Lucas.

"Indeed it is," Eleanor nodded, her gaze drifting to the entrance where Daniel was standing. "Speaking of time, we have a blast from the past joining us tonight."

"Is our Richard also interested in this charming Daniel Thornton ..." also arousing Eleanor's curiosity?

Richard followed her gaze and raised an eyebrow. "Daniel Thornton. I didn't expect to see him here, really."

Eleanor's smile tightened almost imperceptibly. "Neither am I, but he has honored us with his presence. I hope he remembers how to behave in a friendly society."

Lucas, still a journalist, could not resist probing further. "Mrs. Blackwood, what can you tell us about the return of Sir? Thornton?"

Eleanor's eyes rested on Lucas, his expression unreadable. "Not much, I'm afraid. Daniel has always been an enigma, even for his loved ones. Let's focus on the present, not the past. Tonight is the party."Eleanor cut the conversation short.

With that, she turned her attention to another group of guests, leaving Alex and Lucas to ponder over her words.

Alex looked across the room at Daniel, his curiosity piqued. "There is more to his story. I can feel it."

Lucas nodded in agreement. "I'll see what I can dig up".

Alex sipped his champagne. "If there's one thing I've learned, it's that people like Daniel don't come back to Greenwood Hills for no reason."

Lucas smiled, his eyes twinkling with the thrill of the chase. "Don't worry, Alex. Attention is my middle name."

Alex, determined to uncover truth, noted to monitor Daniel all night. In a place of secrets and smiles, every newcomer held a story to uncover.

The grand ballroom, with all its splendor, was just the beginning. Tonight, Alex intended to delve deeper into the mysteries that lurk beneath the surface, understand the true reason for Daniel Thornton's return and navigate the delicate network of relationships and secrets that has defined the elite of Greenwood Hills.

As the evening wore on, Alex drifted through the conversations, his mind half engaged. He exchanged pleasantries with familiar faces, his eyes scanning the room out of habit. The grand ballroom, with its opulence and grandeur, resembled a stage where each player had a role to play. Glasses clattered, voices murmured, creating a soothing hum. Yet, Alex felt something was amiss.

He noticed Daniel once more, talking to Richard. The sight of his father in the middle of discuss Daniel piqued Alex's curiosity. Richard's muscles were coiled like springs, his calm facade crumbling under the weight of unease. Daniel seemed calm and collected, his posture relaxed as he listened.

Intrigued, Alex moved closer, weaving through the crowd with proven ease. As he approached, he caught snatches of their dialogue, their voices merging into the surrounding noise.

" ... important for the family," Richard was saying in a serious and insistent tone. It's crucial that everything goes.

"I understand," Daniel replied, his voice calm and assured. I'm here to assist however I can.

Alex felt an uneasiness. There was something about Daniel that unsettled him, a feeling that he couldn't quite shake. He monitored him throughout the evening, to observe and, perhaps, better understand his true intentions.

As the conversation continued, Richard's expression softened, although the tension remained.

"I appreciate that, Daniel. Good to see you again, but much has changed since your last stay.

Daniel nodded, a slight smile playing on his lips. "I am aware. I'm going to make sure I walk."

Before Alex could hear any more, a hand touched his shoulder. He turned to see Margaret, his expression a mixture of concern and curiosity. "Alex, here you are. I was looking for you. You all right?"

Alex forced a smile by nodding his head. "Yes, Mom, I'm fine. Just... taking it all in."

Margaret glanced at Richard and Daniel, her eyes narrowing. "What's going on over there?"

"I'm not sure," Alex admitted, lowering his voice. "But I intend to find out."

Margaret sighed, her gaze softening as she looked at Alex. "Just be careful. This evening holds significance for us all. We cannot afford any disruption."

"I know," Alex assured her. "I'll take care of it."

As Margaret walked away to join the other guests, Alex turned her attention to Richard and Daniel. The conversation ended, and Richard navigated the crowd, his expression professional once more. Daniel stayed near the entrance, his eyes scanning the room as if he were evaluating the players in a match.

Determined to find out more, Alex approached Daniel, his heart beating. "Mr. Thornton," he greeted, holding out his hand. "I don't believe we had the pleasure. I'm Alex Karter."

Daniel turned around, his piercing green eyes fixed on Alex. For a moment there was an unreadable expression in his gaze, then he smiled, taking Alex's hand. "Alex, of course." I've heard a lot about you.meeting is a pleasure.

"The pleasure is mine," Alex replied, his voice firm. "Welcome to Greenwood Hills. I realize you were away for a while.

Daniel nodded, his smile never wavering. Indeed, it has been several years.

Alex's curiosity remained. "It is. I hope your return will be pleasant."

"So far, so good," Daniel said, releasing Alex's hand. This evening is an event. Eleanor surpassed herself."

"She always does," Alex nodded, glancing around the room. What brings you back to Greenwood Hills after all these years?"

Daniel's smile flickered for a split second, so fast that Alex almost missed him. "Family matters, above all. I felt the need to reconnect and see the changes.

Alex nodded, feeling that there was more to the story. I hope you find what you're searching for.

Parting ways, Alex sensed Daniel's hidden secret. The man's return to Greenwood Hills seemed too fortuitous and his interactions too calculated. Determined to find out the truth, Alex resolved to keep a close eye on Daniel all evening.

The gala continued, the conversations merging into the background of the music, making an almost unique sound. The evening had a new urgency for Alex. In a secretive city, Daniel Thornton's return was a puzzling enigma. Alex was determined to be the one to do it.

Alex was having yet another conversation. But his mind was elsewhere, returning to Daniel Thornton and the disturbing aura he seemed to carry with him. Daniel seemed aware of a secret, unknown to everyone else. The weight of knowledge made Alex feel on the verge of discovering truth.

As the evening progressed, the large ballroom emptied. The guests, sated with refined food and drinks, said their goodbyes, their laughter and their chatter fading into the night. The orchestra played a beautiful last piece, its notes lingering in the air like a bittersweet farewell.

Alex stood by the large windows overlooking the dark grounds of the country club. Reflecting the ballroom chandeliers danced on the glass, casting an almost ethereal glow. The feeling lingered, hinting at a significant prelude.

"Ready to go?"Lucas's voice came through Alex's reverie, bringing him back to the present. Lucas had a keen sense of timing, always knowing when Alex needed a reality check.

"Yeah," Alex nodded, taking one last look at the grand ballroom. "Let's go."

They headed for the exit, the fresh night air a welcome relief after the heat and intensity of the ballroom. Night sounds surrounded them as they stepped outside - crickets chirping, leaves rustling in the breeze. A stark contrast from the opulence they left.

Lucas looked at Alex, a curious gleam in his eyes. "You seemed pretty deep in your thoughts there. Is everything all right?"

Alex shrugged his shoulders, trying to get rid of the persistent discomfort. "Just a lot in my mind. Did you notice how Daniel Thornton seemed to watch everything? It's like he's sizing up the entire room."

Lucas affirmed Alex's thoughts. "Yeah, I saw that. There's something wrong with him, my journalist intuition!

As they made their way to the parking lot, Alex glanced over at the country club, its grandeur looming in the night sky. "I can't help but think that tonight was just the beginning. It feels like something significant is imminent.

Lucas spoke, devoid of any humor in his gaze. "Welcome to Greenwood Hills, where secrets are as deep as pockets. We'll figure it out, Alex. We always do."

The last ones to leave the gala had left his parents on their side. They reached Lucas's car, and Alex slipped into the passenger seat, the cold leather against the fabric of his suit. As they walked away, the lights of the country club moved away, replaced by the quiet streets. Alex looked out the window, his mind racing with unanswered questions and a sense of impending change.

Everyone was lost in their own thoughts as silence filled the way home. When they stopped at the Carter Mansion, Alex turned to Lucas. "Thank you for tonight. I needed company."

Lucas smiles, a genuine warmth in his eyes. "Any time, Alex. We're in this together."

Alex watched Lucas drive away, feeling that his life was about to transform. The serene surface was about to be shattered, revealing the complex and often tumultuous lives below. He took a deep breath, preparing himself for everything that awaited him.

The night was quiet, almost unnerving, as Alex walked up the steps leading to his house. He stopped at the door, taking one last look at the dark street. A premonition settled on him, but also a determination. Whatever secrets Greenwood Hills held, he was ready to discover them.

Entering the house and closing the door, he realized this was just the start of a life-altering journey, reshaping his understanding of his city, family, and self. And despite the uncertainty, Alex felt a spark of determination. He was ready to face whatever came next.

CHAPTER 2

THE SHOCKING DISCOVERY

The chaos engulfed the serene city as screaming sirens illuminated the green alleys. Emergency services occasionally disrupt the upscale neighborhoods' daily life. This morning, the police cars that intersected at the crossroads agitate the alarm clock.

A shower of texts scattered to the closest announce with a brief message the unimaginable tragedy. One day, more like the others, the terrible news broke the beau of yesterday's gala.

At the foot of the grand staircase, disarticulated and with her limbs out of alignment, Eleanor Blackwood's lifeless body lay in the property's heart, her elegant crumpled dress now a reminder of the violence that shattered the tranquility of yesterday evening. As the horror unfolded, the grandeur of the ballroom, once filled with laughter and music, became a stark contrast, now emptied and filled by death, yet the festive spirit still soared.

The police car blocking the front of the property showed that the rescue service and city police had arranged an impromptu parking lot for their flashing cars.

Detective Sarah Mitchell took matters into her own hands, her presence commanding immediate attention. She was a seasoned investigator, known for her pragmatic approach and sharp instincts. Together with a team of officers, she secured the morbid scene, collecting the first statements from the household staff. His piercing eyes lacked nothing, scrutinizing every detail in search of clues that could unravel the mystery of Eleanor's untimely death.

"Everyone, please stay calm," Mitchell's voice echoed above the whisper. "We need to secure the area and gather as much information as possible.

A black lacquered car arriving in a rush. The dust sprayed on the luxurious carcass braked by a police officer, letting Alex out. Tracking Lucas,

Alex stood with Lucas planted, the image of Eleanor's body imagined by the figure that the cover suggested and her tangled hair protruded.

Richard and Margaret arrived at the scene with their faces decomposed, Margaret depicted in makeup, holding on to each other for support. The sight of his parents' distress fueled Alex's determination to find out what had happened.

"Alex," Richard said, his voice low and urgent, his eyes fixed on his son's. "We must cooperate with the investigation. Stay calm and answer all the questions they ask."

Alex feeling the weight of his father's words. He glanced at Lucas, who was already taking mental notes, his journalistic instincts kicking in. Lucas's eyes were sharp, taking in every detail, every reaction, as he prepared to unravel the story behind the tragedy.

Luca intends to use his notes for the Karter family.

"Detective Mitchell!" Richard called, getting his attention. "This is my son, Alex, and his friend Lucas Bennett. They might have useful information for your investigation."

Mitchell approached them, his expression serious but professional. "Thank you, Mr. Karter."

"Mr. Alex Karter, Mr. Lucas Bennett, I need to ask you both a few questions about the events that led to Ms. Blackwood's death."

Alex took a deep breath, steadying himself. "Of course, inspector. We will help you in any way we can."

Mitchell with his pen resting on his notebook. Begin with what you witnessed last night. "Did any of you notice anything unusual, or did someone act?"

Alex exchanged a look with Lucas before answering. "Not especially. The Gala was a great success organized by Eleanore. We were both monitoring Mr. Daniel Thornton. His return caused a lot of speculation, and he was involved in several intense conversations in the evening, including one with Eleanor."

Mitchell's eyes narrowed. "Daniel Thornton, you say? Interesting. What can you tell me about his interactions with Mrs. Blackwood?"

Lucas interposed, his voice calm and measured. "We saw them talking. They appeared engaged in a serious discussion, but we were unable to hear the conversation. Daniel's presence tonight was remarkable. He seemed to watch everyone closely."

Mitchell noted their statements, his expression thoughtful. "Thank you. It's useful. I need to talk to Mr. Thornton as soon as possible."

As she turned to continue her investigation, Alex felt a hand on her shoulder. It was Tori, her face pale and her eyes wide with fear. "Alex, what are we going to do? It's a nightmare."

Tori collapsed sobbing, hugged the circumference of Alex's torso only a few meters from her mother. A police officer intervenes to reinforce the security cordon of the scene.

Alex, "We'll be fine, Tori," Alex said, trying to be reassuring despite the turmoil inside of him. "Inspector Mitchell seems very competent. She'll know what happened."

Tori, although her expression, remained troubled. "I can't believe this is happening. The next day..."

"I know," Alex whispered. "But we have to stay strong. For Eleanor, and for everyone here."

As the day brightened the large rooms, the ballroom remained a controlled stage. The once bustling atmosphere was now heavy with fear and uncertainty. The scientific teams invest every square centimeter. Alex and Lucas were moving in front of the few people present.

"Someone here knows more than he's letting on," Lucas said, his eyes scanning the room. "We just have to figure out who."

Alex's determination hardening. "We will. But we must be careful. The culprit is there, keeping a close eye on those who come near the truth.

As the hours passed, Detective Mitchell continued her interviews, her methodical approach bringing a sense of order to the investigation. The additions can leave, but not until they are ordered to stay for more questioning.

Richard and Margaret found Alex and Lucas near the exit, their expressions tired but resolute.

"It's not over," Richard said. "We must remain vigilant. More is at stake than our family's reputation. We were all present at this gala."

"Okay," Alex murmured, his mind spinning from the night's events. "We will understand it."

Leaving the country club, the morning rays failed to warm their hearts. Alex felt a disgust and an inner strength that gives him this determination to explore the truth. The serene facade of the battered city. Reflecting on the grand entrance, he realized their truth-seeking journey resembled a blackboard.

As Alex made his way to his car, he resolved to face the challenges that awaited him, determined to do justice to Eleanor and restore a sense of peace in the community he called home. Lucas stayed by her side, his own mind buzzing with the potential story. The journalist in him was already piecing the story together, but the friend in him was worried about Alex. Together, they stood, observing shocked faces that had fled the portal.

Alex sighed, his mind racing. "Eleanor's death was not an accident, and we can't sit by and do nothing."

Lucas "You're right. But we must be careful. Luca shared his initial opinion on Eleanor's death, warning that the perpetrator may create additional danger.

"I know," Alex replied, determination hardening his voice. "But we can't let fear stop us. The truth must be known in this city. We won't allow a media rumor to taint the KARTER family's reputation. You understand yourself, Lucas! You are a journalist. "

Alex joins the family nucleus in the mansion, Richard and Margaret Karter as unarmed in the father's large office. Alex's shirt was open, Margaret had a pale complexion, and Richard sat behind his imposing old desk as if only his desk was always there to accompany him under all circumstances.

Richard sent this question: "My son, how are you feeling?"

"I'm fine," Alex replied, although the Gala went well. Let's discuss what occurred. We underestimate the complexity of the situation.

Richard's expression made his eyelids wrinkle and his eyebrows raise. "Let's go inside things. We need to discuss our next steps."

Inside the manor, the familiar environment provided a momentary feeling of comfort. The majestic, extinguished fireplace gave an empty and cold atmosphere by accusing Eleanor of lifelessness.

Richard in an authoritative tone "This case has gone wrong. Greenwood Hills resembles a village during scandals. "We have already paid a lot for it."

Our lawyer will contact the press service.

"All right," Margaret added, her voice soft but firm. "

Alex finally let go of the suspicion he had since the gala evening.

"We need to examine Daniel Thornton. His involvement in the mysterious events rules out coincidence. We require further information on the Blackwood family's tensions.

"I grant you Alex, but I beg you to be as discreet as possible," Richard warned. Let's avoid drawing attention and associating with drama. Alex, go back to KARTER finance as soon as you can. I understand your pain."

Alex realized that belonging to a big rich family made him carry more than his current financial affairs on his shoulders.

He thought of Daniel Thornton and a hidden link with his father may exist. He thought of Eleanor's announcement and the hidden tensions they might have revealed. Above all, he remembered Eleanor lying by the stairs.

Later that day, Inspector Sarah Mitchell goes to the KARTERS' home. Later that day, Inspector Sarah Mitchell, a woman with a powerful charisma and high respect in her investigation department and hierarchy, investigated at the KARTERS' home.

Waiting outside the front door to interrogate the KARTERS.

Authentic passages of this family imbue the places here, not worn out. In no way impressed by this opulent architectural environment common in these neighborhoods. Mitchell coming from the most popular neighborhoods on the EAST Coast.

The housekeeper of the KARTERS, as if padding it with armor, opened the wide door of wood and thick glass. To think how this tiny little housekeeper can exert her strength to activate this fortified panel.

Conducted in a room, acting as a buffer between strangers and dialogue.

A generational protocol, perpetual in the KARTER DNA.

Mitchell started straight, shoulder straightened by its arch, observed the room as if it had already established a first interrogation with the environment

"Inspector! " Exclaimed Alex, who was even more delighted to see him again and thought that the investigation was speeding up."

Mitchell said, "Mr. Carter."

Alex, with a wave of his arm, invites the host to settle down in one choice of well-equipped sofas surrounding a coffee table supporting an object that will be "Art".

Mitchell," Mr. KARTER," she said, renewed her plan for his visit.

"I thank you for making yourself available for the investigation." I have, as you must know, some additional questions concerning the death of Mrs. Blackwood.

Alex throwing with an explicit gesture his agreement.

Mitchell asked, "What was your relationship with Mrs. Blacklood?" Mr. KARTER, I request your personal answer, not the viewpoint of your family. »

Alex likes his question-and-answer exercises. He is a seasoned business executive.

Alex said, "Eleanor was like a second mother to me." Her kindness was unmatched in Greenwood Hills. My closeness to Tori, her daughter, has strengthened our bonds over the years. Sometimes Tori would invite me to dinner, as Eleanor enjoyed hosting.

Mitchell by highlighting his scribbles. Have you had any business dealings together?

Alex asks for a clarification, "With Tori or Eleanor?"

Mitchell said, "maybe both?" answer me, Mr. KARTER.

Alex, "We've never thought about it, maybe joking or at least quipping. We still managed to conduct some business at KARTER finance. Alex took a sip of saliva.

The inspector marked a time-out,

Mitchell's circular head movement traces the angles of the walls. "Don't you think that your gigantic walls have big ears?"

What to understand about this question? Alex sought the depths of the inspector's thoughts. He marked a time, a pause.

"Inspector," Alex said again, "where are you getting at?"

"Mitchell," said Jute, "I have a few routine questions for Mr. KARTER."

Alex, with an almost nervous air, says, "Listen, Inspector Mitchell. Both you, as a police officer, and I, as Alex Karter, a member of the Karter branch and shareholder operator of Karter Finance, want to establish the truth." Eleanor was very dear to my heart, and as I told you, Tori, her daughter, we were very connected. Tori is a lawyer and many times she has helped me to unravel conflicting files. "

Alex advised, "I suggest searching other people's homes, like Thornton's. He's like a tick, you know, the insect in our valleys!"

Mitchell bounces back on Alex's words. "Do you have any 'heavy' against Mr. Daniel Thornton?"

"Heavy! yes, it's a stopover! Alex announced to the inspector.

Mitchell said, "We must warn you about your relationships revolving around your family, Mr. KARTER."

Alex confidently affirmed, "Yes, that's correct." "

Mitchell felt amazed. "Your father?"

Alex said, "Yes, my father had an exchange with Daniel during this evening, an exchange that my ears couldn't even remember the snippets."

Mitchell, "Are they in business?

Alex replied, "not that I know", someone will have informed me. I am in business with my father through our company.

Alex says, "Inspector Mitchell, I am counting on you for total discretion while I solve this disgusting crime. You understand I have important business to run."

With a pout while listening to Alex, Mitchell raises his questions again. "A crime, Mr. KARTER

Alex, "Eleanor couldn't fall off the stairs. We both drank a lot of champagne, but we weren't drunk. "

Mitchell, "Mr. KARTER, it will be up to us to judge whether a murder or an accident caused the death; thank you Mr. KARTER."

Alex, "Please".

Alex's parents stayed away from this interrogation. Richard has always been the protective patriarch, or rather protector of his important financial affairs.

The housekeeper, as well as when she arrived, escorted inspector Mitchell back.

No downtime to operate the KARTER finance entity. The next day, Alex joined his position as shareholder; He spent the morning on the phone. Behind the glass panels, a lone man realized he had a second task after Eleanor's death - conducting a parallel investigation alongside the police.

"Hello, Lucas. This is Alex." How're you doing? The mobile phone resting on the ledge of the panoramic window, his earphone in his ear peering into the vague horizon line.

Lucas asked, "Are you better, Alex?

Alex, Yes Thank you. How about you? Do you have anything new?"

Lucas, "The investigation has just begun. Mitchell probed me! " He exclaimed!"

"Are you ready to step up a gear, Alex?"

Alex sees in his question an affirmation and his impatience.

Alex "This morning I already put a retired friend of the FBI on the spot. He will help us. Lucas, have you confronted others about Daniel? Who else noticed Daniel that night? Did Lucas see someone at Eleanore's house or did someone return there?

Lucas said, "These tracks belong to Alex."

Alex asked. "I'm going to help Tori with the funeral. Do you want to be there?"

Lucas is a friend, and a faithful committed. He quickly answered at the phone's end. He also thinks that the next few days and during the funeral, thinking the journalist will unearth additional elements.

Alex's first stop was the Greenwood Hills Historical Society, a majestic building that housed archives of the city's past and its eminent personalities. People knew the Historical Society for its meticulous archives, which were a treasure trove of information for anyone willing to dig deep enough. Alex spent hours reviewing financial statements and records of Eleanor's philanthropic activities and business ventures. He scrutinized each document, looking for any signs of embezzlement or suspicious transactions.

As he delved deeper into the files, Alex reconstructed a picture of Eleanor's financial transactions. She had taken part in many projects, ranging from real estate to charitable foundations. Alex observed some unusual transactions in his businesses-large sums of money shifting between accounts with minimal explanation. It was a lead, although tentative.

Lucas frequented the city's social hotspots, conversing with acquaintances of Eleanor's. It began at the Greenwood Hills Country Club, where many of the city's elites gathered. The club's opulent setting contrasted with the members' gloomy mood, still reeling from the previous night's events.

Lucas approached a group of women known for their close ties with Eleanor. "Excuse me, ladies," he began, flashing his most charming smile.

"I'm Lucas Bennett, journalist. I'm looking into Eleanor's life and trying to figure out what happened. Anything you could share about him would be invaluable."

The women exchanged suspicious glances before the bolder of the two spoke up. "Eleanor was involved with Councilman Harris. It was more than business; there were rumors of an affair and devious agreements. When things went south, it got ugly. They had a public argument, and many thought it would ruin her, but she bounced back. Still, there were whispers that Harris never forgave him."

Lucas asked, trying to conceal his eagerness. Is there a connection to his death?"

The woman shrugged her shoulders. "Who knows? So many secrets exist in this city. But Eleanor had the gift of making powerful enemies."

Armed with this new information, Lucas went to Alex's office. The weight of their discoveries hanging in the air, the gravity of the situation, became more apparent.

"I found something big," Alex began, spreading out the documents he had copied.

"These transactions-money moves between accounts without a rational purpose. Some of it even goes offshore. It looks like she was laundering money."

Lucas' eyes widened as he scanned the documents. "And I found out that she was involved in a scandal with Councilman Harris. It was more than business; there were rumors of an affair and shady business."

"Do you think Harris could be involved?" Alex asked, his mind racing with the implications.

"It's possible," Lucas replied. "He had a motive, and if Eleanor was blackmailing him or threatening his career, he could have seen her as a threat that needed to be eliminated."

Pieces were falling, yet gaps remained. Eleanor's financial dealings and her involvement with powerful Greenwood Hills figures painted a picture of a woman who had played a dangerous game and paid the ultimate price. But who had delivered the final blow?

"We need to talk to Councilman Harris," Alex said, determination in his voice. "And we need to dig deeper into these financial files. If Eleanor was laundering money, someone had to know about it."

Lucas nodded. "All right. But shouldn't we talk to Detective Mitchell about it? If we are correct, we are dealing with individuals who will go to any lengths to safeguard their secrets.

In a firm tone, Alex pushes the directive, "Let's go visit this Daniel. Let's see what he has in his guts! "

Lucas said, "I feel like I'm hearing your father's voice."

Alex, "About this I took a step back and vigilance, my father knows Councilman Harris."

Two men looked and saw Daniel Thornton in the doorway, his face tense. The once confident man now appeared desperate.

"I heard you were investigating Eleanor's murder," Daniel said, his voice low and urgent.

Alex, "I need to talk to you."

Daniel had his furniture installed on a covered part, adjusting his house. Scattered furniture, books and press clippings leave on the table. An open cigar box stuck to his laptop closed him.

This space served as an office for Daniel, creating a tobacco-filled atmosphere. A cat was making its way to the exit near a reed bed that obstructed the neighbor's view.

"Come in," Daniel said, pointing to an empty chair. Share your thoughts with us.

"I know I've been the subject of a lot of speculation," Daniel began, his voice firm but tense. "And I won't deny that my return to Greenwood Hills has stirred things up. But I need you to understand that I am not your enemy."

Lucas leaned forward, his eyes narrowing. "Then why are you here, Daniel? What do you know about Eleanor's murder?"

Daniel sighed, his shoulders sagging. "Eleanor and I had a complicated relationship. We were business partners, and yes, we had our disagreements. But I respected her. She was ruthless, but she was also fair. The scandal you're talking about involves Councilman Harris. Eleanor found out that he was involved in illegal activities-money laundering, corruption. She threatened to expose him."

Alex's eyes widened. The pieces were falling into place. "So Eleanor was blackmailing Harris? And he retaliated?"

Daniel. "it was more than that. Harris is part of a larger network. Powerful people with a lot to lose. Eleanor's death was more than just silencing her.

"Did you say murder?" asked Alex.

Daniel wondered, "Do you think she tripped on her stairs?"

Lucas's mind raced. "And you, Daniel? Where do you stand in all this?"

"I was trying to help Eleanor," Daniel said, his voice filled with sincerity. "I warned her to be careful, to gather more evidence before doing anything. But she was determined, too confident in her ability to handle the situation. Upon my return to Greenwood Hills, my intention was to rectify the situation and uncover the mastermind.

Alex studied Daniel's face, looking for any signs of deception. "Why should we trust you? Are you not involved in this network?"

Daniel met Alex's gaze, his eyes fixed. "Because I'm risking everything by returning to this place." If the people behind Eleanor's murder find out I'm talking to you, they'll come after me, too. Look at this peaceful place! Almost there, but Manhattan still seems far away. "

The room fell silent as Alex and Lucas absorbed Daniel's words. Stakes surpassed expectations, truth's path treacherous.

"We'll need proof," Alex said. "Something concrete that connects Harris and this network to Eleanor's murder. "

Daniel nodded. "I have documents. Evidence that Eleanor gathered before her death during the gala evening was our exchanges. It's not enough to bring them down, but it's a start. Go see Eleanor's library,"

"So let's start there," Lucas said, determination in his voice. The longer we wait, the more dangerous it becomes. "

As they planned their plan, the atmosphere in the room changed from tension to a shared sense of purpose. They were about to discover something monumental, and despite the risks, they were ready to face whatever was coming next.

Daniel looks grave and pained. The confident and calm man now seemed vulnerable, the weight of recent events pressing heavily on him. Alex and Lucas were observing him, feeling that they were about to discover crucial information.

Daniel hesitated for a moment, then continued. "There is more. Eleanor was in contact with a private investigator. She hired him to examine some people she was dealing with. A certain James. He might have more information. "

"James? Lucas repeated and scribbled the name in his notebook. We need to speak with him too.

"We are going to part ways," Alex said. "Lucas and I will go to the family estate and collect the documents. Daniel, you need to find this private investigator and see what he knows. "

Daniel with a frozen face "I'm going to find him. But if someone finds out what we're doing, they won't hesitate to stop us. "

The men disperse, their minds obsessed with Alex, making them forget his role that Alex becomes to play at KARTER finance. His car, phone calls, emails - a productive workday. Alex and Lucas remain surprised by Daniel's confidences.

Lucas wondered if Daniel should have let go of these denials to the police, Alex."

Alex said, "To tell the truth, Lucas, nothing surprises me anymore, you know." Since Eleanor's murder, I've been feeling jaded."

The men swallow their still hot cup of coffee in the car. An almost automatic mechanical gesture that acts as a cerebral fuel.

Sporty driving, Alex wants to shorten the time of the distances traveled that seemed unbearable to him. These imposing hands clasp the steering wheel of the car, arms outstretched. He executes his driving like a pilot.

Arrived at Eleanor's deserted house occupied only by a servant, yellow garlands of the police were the vestiges of memory of the horror.

The two friends showed exaggerated empathy towards the servant and thanked her for welcoming them, despite the instructions of the officials still prohibiting access to the premises.

She prepares them a coffee arranged on a silver tray, a jar of sugar, a jar of milk cream. The cups were of a great finish as a gold border encircled the edge.

"Here, gentlemen, served in Mrs. Blackwood's favorite coffee service," she said in a faltering voice. "If you need, you ring me at this button."

The companions, Alex and Lucas, see this as an opportunity to infiltrate Eleanor's small office.

"This room is a real cramped mess," Alex said

"Like this case," Lucas replied

"Where are these documents supposed to be?

"Lucas whispered, his voice was audible in the silence."

"In Eleanor's office," Daniel had said. Behind a fake sign in the library. "

They found the office, its big wooden doors creaking as they pushed them open. As they pushed open the big wooden doors, the room greeted them with the smell of aged leather and dust, and the shelves towered over them.

"Here," Lucas said. "Is this painting your father's portrait?! "

Alex was dumb and stunned to see his father's painting hanging in this enigmatic room.

"Another gift from my father. He liked to distribute gifts at all times," Alex's Calm tone notes that his father often watered his network with gifts of all kinds.

Lucas rummaged around the edges, and with a silent click, the panel opened to reveal a hidden compartment. Inside were stacks of documents, organized and labeled.

"Jackpot," Lucas breathed, removing the files. "Let's hand them over to your office in a safe place."

Alex, "Let's greet the servant, and thank her."

Meanwhile, Daniel has tracked down James, the private investigator. He found it in a dingy office in the less affluent part of the city. Despite his worn-out appearance, the man's eyes remained sharp and alert. The ambient smell seemed familiar to him but a unique brand of cigar than those that Daniel smoked.

"James? "Daniel asked as he came inside."

"Who wants to know?" James replied, giving him a suspicious look.

"Eleanor Blackwood hired you," Daniel said, getting straight to the point. "I am his nephew. I need to know what you found. "

James studied Daniel for a while. "All right, come in. But it will not be easy. Eleanor was on to something big. "

Daniel and James discussed the investigation, while Alex and Lucas sorted through recovered documents at the office.

"Look at this," Alex said, holding up a folder. "It's a list of names and transactions. Eleanor dealt with these individuals. If we can link them to financial irregularities, we may have enough to eliminate them. "

Lucas's eyes scanning the pages. "It's more than interesting. "

They were getting closer to the truth and, with each additional proof, they felt the momentum being created.

Lucas "It's a real puzzle. You like it Alex. I know you like to unravel complicated cases."

"Lucas, always speak!" you the journalist! His side smile brought back his charisma as a mature man.

A noise of three well-adjusted shots interrupts their bubble of investigators. Alex's office door is knocked twice more.

Alex said, "Yes, please come in!"

The door opens, letting slip forward a pretty cutthroat face that emerges from a neckline. Using one finger, the young woman raises her glasses and says,

"Mr. Karter, your father tried to reach you, so did I."

Alex asked, "Did he leave a message?"

He will join the council shortly, Sir.

Alex "Then remind him to tell him to confirm my presence, too. Sorry, I forgot this advice."

"Good, Mr. KARTER," she said, closing the door almost on her tapering face.

"An extraordinary piece of advice? "Lucas wonders

"Nothing extraordinary. My father wishes to 'lull' the investors since this case. "

"I'm leaving Alex. I'll see you another moment. I don't want Richard to cross my journalist gaze!"

Alex "We are Lucas, and thank you. "

Alex cleared the table to make room for these papers in his archives.

He's getting back to his job as a good financial executive.

Almost also, Richard enters his office as his business executive's assistant. Business executives made a remark, skipping the usual pleasantries. The voice roque,

"It is dark here! Have you seen the sun outside? "

"Hello dad, from the sun, yes," retorts Alex

Richard, "I see you have immersed yourself in business. Is that right, my son? Stay the course, ready for the council meeting? "

Alex, "If you haven't changed the agenda, then yes, I'm ready."

Richard smashes a key on the intercom of Alex's office phone.

"Astrid, please give the file of the new agenda to Mr. Alex Karter" His directness voice activated, acting the assistant that the two business managers share.

Alex looks at the printed folder. A silence punctuates the exchanges.

"What does this update mean, dad? "Alex surprised e taken lessons

"My son, considering the period that has weakened in Greenwood Hills, our city! I wanted to rmean,eassure our shareholders by proposing substantial reinjections."

"Hmm... Let's see this at the hearing. Dad, you're in the majority. Do you think that will be enough? We are unaware of the remaining events surrounding Eleanor's death.

Let's always challenge Alex's perspective. It is for you I am doing this. You are my successor and wish to protect our 'family jewel."

"About protecting dad, have you done the necessary for Eleonor's case? »

Alex, I partitioned everything and focused on network levers.

Alex felt his father's hand take possession of the circumference on his neck. Often, his patriarchal gesture annoyed Alex. He never pushed back for fear that his father would think that Alex opposed this archaic ritual and was too cavalier for his taste.

Alex is not one to be tactile with others, even with his loved ones. Kiss the champagne glass, like Eleanor did at the Gala. Those eyes shine in the vague. Richard startled him.

"We're waiting for you, Alex, in the big room." He looks at his thick watch that exceeds his wrist circumference. "In 10mins, I'm counting on you."

Pensive, since the information dropped from his father. One name, one name too many: Harris.

Alex understood the poor mix of finance and politics, refusing to collaborate with a label given by a clan instead of a network. "

Richard convinced the partners and investors, a well-crafted presentation as his team by his business lawyer, to know how to do it well.

A moment of relaxation was necessary before enduring the funeral. How about friends sharing a drink at their beloved private club near Greenwood Hills? This club used to attract customers from the neighboring county who did a mix of genres.

In these nocturnal places, the music camouflages the obsolete discussions of the partygoers. The colored lights contrast on the dark backgrounds of the VIP seats. Women transform into medusa, wearing heat-resistant outfits. friendly.

Alex appreciates these light and dark places of celebration, but without being attracted by the dance floor. Women often make themselves noticed by Alex, but do not dare to cross an invisible line Alex draws from his powerful personality.

In a VIP box designed for prestigious clients, two men in casual attire always take their positions.

Lucas crouched to examine the computer. "A shell company? This is a classic gesture to hide illegal activities. Can you find the owners? "

"I'm working on it," Alex replied, his fingers hovering over the keyboard. "But it's difficult. These things are as opaque as possible. "

These names represent processing agents for the source client.

Lucas's eyes widened. "Why are there several names of treatment agent? "

Alex said, "Let me explain." I've gone through the documents. There is a complete list of dubious transactions in particular. This sounds like a massive fund fraud scheme. We need to understand how they set up these operations and who is involved.

Lucas: "Okay, show me what you found. Look, this first series of transactions reminds me of the Panama Papers case where millions of dollars hid in tax havens."

Alex: "Yes. I have noticed that several of these transactions use shell companies, similar to those discovered in the Mossack Fonseca case. Eleanor used nominees to conceal the real beneficiaries of the funds."

Lucas: "It's a classic modus operandi. It looks like she exploited loopholes in international banking regulations. What intrigues me are these transfers to Swiss and Cayman Islands accounts. Harris could be involved. He had both the access and means to orchestrate this. "

Alex: "You're right, Harris had the contacts. Even more disturbing is that some transfers date back years, when my father, Richard, had 80% of Karter Finance shares. I wonder if he wasn't involved from the beginning. "

Lucas: "We need to check that out. Richard's involvement could explain Eleanor's ability to act without detection. Maybe he used his position at Karter Finance to cover his tracks, a bit like that painting that kept the documents at their place. " Analyze account connections to determine Richard's involvement in other suspicious transactions.

Alex: "I've already started doing cross-checks. Similar to the Bernie Madoff case, they redistributed the funds to hide the losses. Eleanor seems to have created a similar system, a kind of international Ponzi scheme. "

Lucas: "That makes sense. If she has set up a Ponzi scheme, it would explain the constant movement of funds to pay investors with newcomers' money. We need to identify the victims and understand the extent of the damage. "

Alex: "I'm going to contact forensic accounting experts to analyze the financial documents. We also need to coordinate with the international authorities, FBI. We need to coordinate with international authorities, such as the FBI, as this type of fraud, like the Enron, involves embezzling hundreds of millions of dollars. "

Lucas: "Good idea. Let's also make sure we keep our communications secure. Harris or Richard's involvement might dampen our spirits. "

Alex: "Perfect. I will start by compiling all the evidence and preparing a detailed report. Let's monitor Harris' movements for any signs of hidden funds or attempts to flee. "

Lucas: "I'm going to focus on Richard's lead. You, his son, remain behind him. If we can prove his involvement, this could be the key to dismantling the entire fraud network. We need to be thorough and investigate every detail. "

Alex: "The answer to who Eleonor's criminal is remains unresolved"

Alex and Lucas remain silent and realize their presence in this club. All observers inspiring these elites who come here to show themselves but above all to anesthetize their memory of their heavy day.

Behind a smoke screen materialized by rays of spots, Mitchell's silhouette emerges. A police officer in a nightclub...

Lucas chases his foot to hit Alex's, then a shoulder kick.

"Alex, look who's coming here," he says with his pursed lips, as if trying a ventriloquist technique.

"Inspector! What a surprise! »

Mitchell said, "The surprise for you might be Mr. Karter."

"On duty? "Alex entangled

"Perceptive in your intuitions, Mr. KARTTER. You blew me away. "A slight ironic mocking smile from the police officer gave in this evening atmosphere another facet of this official on duty.

"It will be brief," she affirms in a dry tone

"Mr. KARTER, Mr. Bennett, you have crossed the forbidden lines of a police area of an ongoing investigation at Mrs. BLACKWOOD's house."

"And so? "retort Lucas

Mitchell, "Either your little VIP party is ending now for you. I'm taking you on board. Can you spit me out? What were you doing? Usually, criminals return to the scene of their failed crimes.

Friends exchange crossed glances,

Alex "Heard Detective Mitchell, let's go talk in my car. I don't like unnecessary noise here anymore."

Dark and opaque tinted windows door by the night covered with low clouds, the lighting of the ceiling of the car suffices to illuminate the faces. Lucas is standing in the backseat, Mitchell is in the front passenger's chair. Alex puts his laptop between the two and shows the elements collected over the past few hours.

Mitchell said, "Gentlemen, this is evidence withholding."

Alex speeds up the answer. "No more for a few minutes. "

Mitchell, "By these elements, you suspect your own father, Eleanor and Harris. Are you aware of the consequences? I know you have an excellent lawyer, Mr KARTER, but you are jeopardizing your interests that you have with your father."

"Inspector, today my interest with Lucas and even Daniel is to shed light on who may have murdered Eleanor."

Mitchell, "It's the police of the department who will shed light on what you called 'a crime'. I insist on your collaboration, but in no case you come to walk on my flower beds, even less the press."

Mitchell insists on hearing a response from both men. "Heard! »

A feeble agreement failed to make the car's interior logical.

A slightly late arrival to take possession of his office, Alex rubs shoulders with ease with the common areas of the KARTER finance building. The morning passages occupy less than the elevator.

'Hello Mr Karter, FBI Agent Collins has been here waiting for you since 9am. He wishes to speak with you.'

'Hello Astrid, thank you. Let him in, please. Thank you for the "coffee." A sign of lifting the cup covered with its lid.

Agent Collins shows up in Alex's office with an undeniable presence, an imposing stature, he was about ninety meters tall, with an athletic build that denotes a rigorous physical discipline. Her short, dark brown hair dotted with a few graying strands frames a face with features marked by experience and the harshness of missions.

He wears a discreet but elegant civilian outfit: a perfectly fitted dark navy blue suit, an impeccable white shirt and a soberly tied tie. Her black leather shoes are polished to perfection, adding a finishing touch to her professional appearance. He seems like someone who attaches great importance to details, which is reflected in his neat appearance.

By approaching Alex, He emanates from him an aura of confidence marked by years of service within the FBI. Each movement is precise, measured, not one too many.

When he reaches out to Alex, his grip is firm, testifying to a quiet assurance. His voice, grave and calm, carries a natural authority.

Agent Collins: "Good morning, Mr. Alex Karter. I'm Agent Collins from the FBI. We need to talk about the investigation concerning John. "

His tone is professional, but a glimmer of understanding and determination shines in his eyes. He's not just here to ask questions; he's here to solve this case, to do justice to John, a former colleague.

Alex: "Hello, Agent Collins. I am relieved that the FBI is taking this case into their own hands. Please have a seat. "

Agent Collins: "Thank you. We are taking this investigation seriously, especially since John was a former FBI agent. We have the legal competence to intervene and coordinate investigations with local authorities. I'm here to discuss next steps and gather all your collected information. "

Alex: "Of course. What information are you interested in? "

Agent Collins: "First, we're going to do a thorough forensic examination of John's body. Our specialists in forensic analysis and additional interrogations will bring resources to dig deeper. In addition, we would like to offer you protection, Mr. Karter. Given the circumstances, it is possible that you are in danger. "

Alex: "That's great news about the forensic expertise. Honestly, I experienced a slight sense of restriction due to local resources. Detective Mitchell is doing his best, but he doesn't have the same means as you. As for protection, I had not considered this possibility, but I suppose it is a necessary precaution."

Agent Collins: "We understand. That's why we're going to be working closely with Detective Mitchell. I will need all the research elements that you have put together with Lukas. "

Alex turns to his desk, opens a drawer, and pulls out a thick folder. He hands it to Agent Collins.

"Here is everything we have collected so far about Mrs. Eleanor Blackwood. There is a connection with John's murder. Copying notes, observations, potential leads. Lukas and I spent hours analyzing everything.'

Agent Collins said, "This will be very useful to us. Have you discovered anything concrete that could help identify the person or persons responsible? "

Alex: "We discovered several financial anomalies that could have a connection to Eleanor's investigation. Suspicious money transfers, offshore accounts... This could be a lead. "

Agent Collins: "Interesting. Our analysts will comb through this. I will stay in touch for updates. We are going to do everything in our power to solve this case. "

Alex: "Thank you. "

Agent Collins: "Thank you, Mr. Karter. Your cooperation is essential. If you have any concerns or if you notice anything unusual, contact me immediately. Here is my card. "

Alex: "I won't miss it. Thanks again, Agent Collins. "

Agent Collins gets up and leaves the office, leaving Alex with a renewed sense of satisfaction and hope. The FBI taking over meant things were finally going to move forward meaningfully. Alex felt strengthened, ready to continue his quest for truth and justice for John.

Two men divide, discover their fresh day's workload.

CHAPTER 3

DARK HORIZONS

E leanor's funeral day, the city mourns. On this day, the inhabitants remember the deceased.

The funeral order is diligently observed, with a silence respected even by the slow procession of cars. A continuous seasonal rain gives impressing a wet curtain that is torn by the imposing luxury carcasses.

The local newspaper of Greenwood Hills uncerated in front of Richard seated, in title "BLACKWOOD MURDER", the right arm leaning on the edge of the glass. His face gives off an inert pout, his thoughts freeze, his features marked by his powerful character and his long career, raises his hand close to his chin, holds out his sleeve tightened by a personalized cufflink to scrutinize the time.

'Only 10 o'clock...' he sighs.

'Then you still have 20 minutes to take it upon yourself, Richard', Margaret replies.

Margaret supports Richard especially to avoid exposing his contemptuous character too much in public when he is not in "his game". She wanted to be on the board, but Richard made it clear that changing the company's family structure was unnecessary.

They keep their old couple's car at a distance from the lead car where Tori and Alex are. In a need for comfort in the face of grief, in a space that promotes closeness, Tori lets herself put her temple on Alex's shoulder height, her knees criss-cross as if to look for an emotional lack that she has just lost.

With one hand, Alex, on his mobile phone, focused on managing his brief messages, which allows him to always keep his business life within the company.

A call breaks this intimacy.

'Hello Lukas, how are you?' in a low voice.

"Good job, Alex." What about Yolk's voice seems to come from the outside?

On our way to the venue.

'I have already arrived despite the bad weather on the roads. I believe I am the first one.

Lukas' 'I'm waiting for you outside the entrance'.

Alex, "Okay Lukas'.

The convoy gathers under a more scattered downpour at the entrance to the cemetery. An escort of the staff responsible for the preparation takes the first step by opening the large metal gate of the city cemetery.

The greenish nature cut by the wide alleys, the old trees with their rocky barks dive above, almost caress the roofs of the convoy.

The engines slowness evokes a slow-motion sound, while prayers maintain these graves with care.

Traffic jams fill the cemetery's heart in a row. The convoy stops. Staff and pastor gather at the grave, covered in wet earth and a white tarpaulin. They set up a prefabricated mobile shelter against this unfavorable weather.

Richard plays his grieving part. Alex was aware that it was his appearance of respectability that could conceal his secrets, even though one or two words of comfort seemed genuine.

Richard stood erect, his piercing gaze sweeping the assembly.

During the ceremony, Alex and Lucas exchanged a glance. The presence of Lucas brought a certain assurance to Alex.

Lucas, carrying his umbrella with folded arms, observes the interactions. The man is used to hearing everything and writing the content in his press articles. Perhaps he'll write an essay on paper.

No speeches, only pale faces and some shy tears. Tori, with Alex's support, places a very red rose as her mother liked it in her rose garden on the property.

Together they carry a shovel of earth, then tilt it to slide into the wet mass like a solid rain that hits the oak wood of the coffin.

There, Tori no longer lifts, Alex hooks her arm, surrounds her hips, regains the row. Tori can't hold back her tears mixed with the drops of water sliding on her fair skin.

We said the prayers, laid the flowers, and whispered our last goodbyes. However, for Alex, this day held more significance than mere mourning.

As the guests dispersed,

Who among this mourning crowd dressed in black is the murderer? Could it be a man or a woman?

The killer's profile may also be a sponsor. A professional? These questions must remain due to the many issues at stake.

Further down the driveway, two parked police cars attracted attention. Inspector Mitchell, with a decided step, approaches Alex, who was standing next to Tori, followed by Richard, Margaret and

Lukas. The ceremony's time frowned upon his sighting of approaching police officers in such a circumstance.

Mitchell posts in front of Alex, his gaze cold and determined. The agent by his side, as if warning himself.

"Mr. Alex Karter," Mitchell began, in a firm but respectful voice. "I must inform you that you are under arrest on suspicion of murder associate the death of John Farwell. You can choose to stay silent. Anything you say can and will be used against you in a court of law. You have a right to an attorney. If you cannot afford an attorney, one will be appointed for you."

Alex opened his eyes wide, an expression of disbelief and shock painting over his face. "What? But this is absurd! John is dead!"

Mitchell remained unfazed. "They found John dead in his vehicle early this morning." We believe you are involved."

Richard, hitherto silent, spoke up. "Inspector, there must be a mistake. Alex was with."

Tori, broke away from Alex's arms. 'We were together until morning!'

Margaret, bow your head for approval. "That's right. We were all together, here, preparing for this ceremony. Inspector, how dare you come now! '

Mitchell gazes at Alex. "That's why we have to take him away for questions. The evidence suffices to warrant further investigation."

Lukas, move closer. "You can't take him like that with no concrete proof! This is madness!"

Mitchell then turned to Lukas. "Mr. Bennett, I know you are investigating this case. If you interfere further, I will also arrest you for obstruction of justice."

Richard was surprised to hear that Alex is conducting an investigation. 'Are you investigating, Alex?'

Lukas remains marble.

Alex, still in shock. "I am unsure of what to express." John was my friend. Why suspect me?"

Mitchell makes a 'no trust,' face, as if he's used to this kind of situation. That is the exact thing we need to uncover. Follow us, please."

Margaret burst into tears. Richard embraced her protectively, and Lukas did the same for Tori.

Richard says to Alex, 'I'm sending you my lawyer, Alex!'

Alex, turning to them, looks at Lukas and whispered.

Mitchell motioned to the agent to pass the handcuffs to Alex, who accepted them without resistance. The police officers slowly returned to their vehicle, taking Alex with them, leaving behind one of the largest famous family in Greenwood Hills devastated. Some guests who witnessed this scene evaporate.

At the city police office.

Alex KARTER stood in Detective Mitchell's austere office, his hand clutching his phone. The walls, filled with files and maps, show the officer's overwhelming workload and prolonged investigations. Mitchell slightly stood up behind his desk, his eyes riveted on the elements of the John and

Eleanor file in front of him. Alex sat opposite, trying to contain some annoyance.

Mitchell finally sat down and stared at Alex with an almost haughty look. "Mr. Karter, we need to talk about John's death. The circumstances are disturbing and the evidence points to your indirect, or direct involvement, Mr. KARTER. What do you have to say?"

Alex puts his voice above Mitchell. "John was my friend, Detective. We were working on Eleanor's crime together. We informed you last night with evidence that this is a premeditated murder, possibly by a sponsor.

Mitchell opening the file in front of her. "The report shows that someone attacked him before he lost control." This does not seem like a coincidence. Who do you think wanted to silence him?."

Alex clenched his fists. "We were investigating financial frauds involving local power figures. I trusted John. He could have helped us. I think someone wanted to prevent it."

Mitchell flipped through the documents in front of him. His body had wrestling marks on it. In addition, we found a folder belonging to you on the passenger seat of John's car. How do you explain this?"

Alex straightened up, disbelief mingling with anger on his face. "A file? Detective, it's impossible. I never left a file in his car. Someone must have placed it there to compromise me, or to discourage me! What do you think, inspector...?".

Mitchell's eyes remained locked on Alex. "That might be the case, but it still puts you under serious suspicion. You must grasp the complication this presents for you.

Alex answered with a resolute voice. Inspector, you are fully aware that I am innocent. John and I were like brothers. Find the culprit among those we investigated. I am convinced that someone is trying to trick me into diverting attention."

Mitchell leaned back in his chair, thinking. "And Lukas? He seems to be very involved in this case. Why is he so determined to investigate for himself?"

Alex leaned forward slightly. Lukas, my loyal friend and competent investigative journalist, shares my desire for truth.

Mitchell insists. "If Lukas interferes again, we will also arrest him," Mitchell insists. We must follow the legal procedure."

Alex sighed, aware of the danger. "I understand, Inspector. But please, focus your efforts on those who had a real motive. Every minute lost could allow the murderer to still be at large."

Mitchell weighing his options. "Very well, Mr. Karter. We will continue to investigate. Be aware that we are keeping an eye on you. Any information you could provide would be helpful. Don't cross my line that I am ordering you to now."

Suddenly, a police officer in a suit entered the room with a briefcase. Alex was visibly relieved to see it.

The man confidently introduced himself. "Inspector Mitchell, I am Mr. Henry Thompson, Mr. Karter's lawyer. We need to talk immediately."

Mitchell seemed slightly annoyed by the interruption. "Very well, Mr. Thompson. Take a seat."

Mr. Thompson sat down next to Alex, putting his briefcase on his lap. "I have just realized the charges against my client. Do you have any other heavy charges that justify this theatrical arrest? I would like to remind you we should presume him innocent until proven guilty. It is unacceptable for him to be questioned without the presence of his lawyer."

Mitchell remained impassive. "We are investigating, and the evidence is overwhelming. Mitchell remained impassive and stated, "We are investigating, and the evidence overwhelmingly shows that a file belonging to your client was found in the victim's car."

Mr. Thompson immediately retorted:

"We strongly dispute this evidence. This file is almost empty. Don't make it a case personal inspector. Someone is attempting to frame Mr. Karter. "

Mitchell was fully aware that the lawyer's presence would complicate matters:

"We will continue to investigate, Mr. Thompson. Mr. Karter and other suspects are under close surveillance. Rather dissuade your client from managing his finance business rather than playing detective with his sidekick Mr. Bennett."

Mr. Thompson. "We will cooperate fully, Inspector. But in the meantime, I ask that you release Mr. Karter on bail, under his rights."

Mitchell paused to consider his response. "Mr. KARTER, you are free to leave for now. But stay available for future interrogations. This case is far from being solved."

Alex, relaxed again, got up, followed by his lawyer: "goodbye Inspector," he said with determination.

As they were leaving the office.

Alex walked out of Detective Mitchell's office, his thoughts in a chaotic whirl. The fresh air from outside the clouds of rain dissipated. He took a good breath.

John's police file, with its brutal descriptions and raw photos, haunted his mind.

He kept revisiting the images of John's body as if it were still in front of his eyes, slumped in the driver's seat, his head tilted, his eyes open and empty. The deep cuts on his forehead, the shards of glass embedded in his scalp, the violent bruises on his arms and hands... every detail was a sharp, throbbing pain. The marks of desperate struggle told a story of agony and terror that John had experienced in his last moments.

Rage and sadness were mixed in Alex. That someone could have done this to John tore him apart from the inside. The image of John tied up, beaten, and left for dead in this car obsessed him. The marks on his wrists, witnesses of a brutal ligature, the sharp cuts on the steering cables of the car, all this formed an appalling picture of betrayal and violence.

Alex felt pain, a sickening, but he repressed them, turning his pain into an icy determination. John's death was a warning, a simple message that their enemies were ready to do anything to protect their secrets.

Mr. Thompson interrupts his thoughts, saying, "Can I take you back, Mr. Karter. "

"That's nice, I'll get some fresh air while walking ". In an exhausted voice.

Alex knew that now that there were two cases, two crimes, assassinations and especially several criminals involved, close to his daily life.

Alex preferred to walk after his exit from an unfair interrogation and completely change his mind, seeking to calm his tormented mind. Greenwood Hills had undergone a refreshing transformation because of the recent rains, showcasing a vibrant green spectacle. The trees lining the sidewalks seemed more alive, their leaves sparkling in the rays of the sun. The public gardens, covered with carpets of dense grass and bright flowers grouped in stone beds, exuded a sweet fragrance of damp earth and reborn vegetation.

Alex was grateful for the slight creaking under his steps as he walked down the streets, which still gleamed with traces of humidity. The winds calmed his nerves, carrying away the showers and leaving debris. The beaded rain droplets on the flower petals added a touch of magic to this urban decor. The birds sang happily, as if to celebrate this rebirth of nature, gorged with water to better recharge her batteries, and their melody had a calming effect on her restless mind.

From time to time, a Tudor-style house, with its dark wooden half-timbering and sloping roofs, interrupted the architectural harmony, offering an interesting and picturesque contrast. Alex loved this English Renaissance style, attached to decorum since his internship period in London where he had known these first independence as a young man. Still in training, he had spent a memorable internship in the British capital. A time of discoveries, first independence, and new freedom.

He remembered the cobbled streets of the Kensington district where he was staying, lined with those same Victorian houses with elegant facades and ornate verandas. The foggy mornings, when the London fog enveloped the buildings, gave an almost mystical atmosphere to his daily journeys and those endless rainy days like that day of the funeral ceremony. The mansard roofs and bay windows, so typical of the Victorian style, reminded him of the walks he often took, stopping to admire the architectural details that told so many stories of the past.

During his internship, he had discovered the joys of independence. The cozy pubs where he met his friends after a day's work, the discreet cafes where he read while enjoying tea with his girlfriend Fleur, his first name, in French Fleur means 'flower'. He found it indeed beautiful and pure, like a first spring flower. A pinkish face with light blue eyes, blonde hair with red highlights.

He called her "my pretty heart", when she heard she was straightening her bust, which highlighted her young woman's shapes.

He had since forgotten her last name. Surely she had a very British name!

Love existed, but Alex favored work. Hammered by his severe education, he did not shy away from it, which cultivated this thirst to learn and become a recognized expert in the world of finance.

Green parks, like Hyde Park, offered solace for him to ponder and enjoy the company of ducks, often surpassing the darker aspects of humanity. Hyde Park, sitting on a similar bench, had impeccable lawns. The same sensations of tranquility and renewal that he experienced now in Greenwood Hills.

Alex also remembered the challenges he had faced. Acquiring the skills to navigate in a large foreign city, adjusting to a new professional setting, and, above all, demonstrating to himself his ability to thrive away from home.

Away from his father.

This period had forged him, giving him a confidence in his abilities and a determination that he had never lost.

The memories of his walks through the historic streets of London were vivid. The buildings of the Hampstead district. Alex had learned to listen, to appreciate the richness of the history that surrounded him.

Coming back to the present, Alex recognizes the influential nature of this time for him. The tranquility of Greenwood Hills shaken up since these abominable crimes, the disgust that awakened in him a bittersweet nostalgia.

Wasn't Tori's presence a hidden frustration of a dreamed desire to continue Fleur's long-standing relationship?

Alex loves justice, and can not stand the brakes contrary to his principles.

Justice for the memory of Eleanor and John. He ruminated during this breath of fresh air.

Eventually, he reached a small square with ancient trees and a broken fountain. Alex leaned back against one bench, closing his eyes for a moment, letting the soothing noise calm his mind.

Pausing briefly to reflect on the tranquil scene surrounding him. Children playing.

Alex takes his phone out of his inner jacket pocket and calls Tori, precious friend. After a few rings, she picks up the phone.

"Alex, how are you?" Tori asked, her tone full of concern.

Alex paused briefly before responding, as if readjusting: "Tori, I need to talk to you. Things are getting really complicated. John... Someone killed him. And they're trying to make me wear the hat."

Tori was silent for a moment, assimilating the news: "I'm sorry, Alex. What can I do to help?"

"I haven't made up my mind yet," Alex replied.

"You will not be alone," she said. Discover truth, bring justice to John.

A wave of comfort washed over Alex as he heard her words. "Thank you, Tori. I was confident that I could rely on you. "

Tori asks him with a sudden idea: "Let's have dinner together tonight at the restaurant. It will remind us of our friendly tables with you and mom!"

"Great idea Tori, say 7pm at The Trattoria Verde? "Alex resumed his charismatic smile. A wonderful moment of good company makes him show his strength as a business executive through all tests.

Richard, at his desk in the mansion, finishes the phone call away from the main entrance corridor.

"Ah, Alex! In two steps, three movements! You are familiar with my dear expression! is it not expeditious my lawyer?"

"Indeed, so efficient that it allowed me to enjoy the pretty park of our beautiful city for a while. I haven't been there since ..."

With the smile of a father who reminisces about family memories, he says: "Since your mother took you for a stroll in a stroller! ".

"Ah, Mom... She did everything."

"And your father, he, to finance everything that she has always wanted to do, my son! "Almost exclaimed."

"Our business is good, Alex. Are you at least aware of that?"

"I don't doubt it. Why this question?"

"Tell me, do you speak Spanish, or did you forget your private lessons in Middlebury, in Vermont?"

"I have leftovers thanks to a professional activity," Alex is curious about this question.

One of our investors and South American client is reaching out to us for a subsidiary

Richard: "Alex, do you have a moment for us to discuss an interesting opportunity?"

Alex: "Of course, dad. What is it about?"

Richard: "It's a fact that our client investors in South America are very excited about expanding our business there. They are reaching out to help us set up a subsidiary in this region."

Alex: "A subsidiary in South America? It's an ambitious idea. What advantages do you perceive in this expansion? "

Richard: "South America is a growing market with huge potential. Our local partners have connections and market knowledge that would be invaluable to us. In addition, some countries, such as Panama, offer relatively flexible offshore rules. This could facilitate our international operations and free up more cash to show our strength at KARTER Finance. "

Alex: "Panama, huh? Their offshore rules are average, not as strict as in other countries, but not completely lax either. But it remains a sensitive area. There are often legal and ethical complications to consider. "

Richard: "Absolutely. To minimize tax and legal risks, we must structure our subsidiary accordingly. By using financial tools such as special purpose companies (SPV) and trusts, we will protect our assets while maintaining a certain operational flexibility. This would also allow us to strengthen our cash flow and show our financial robustness. "

Alex: "SPVs and trusts can indeed offer advantages in terms of risk management and tax planning. But we ensure we comply with international regulations and that we do not appear to be exploiting tax loopholes. I am also concerned about the transparency and ethics of our local partners. "

Richard: "Your concerns are legitimate. That is why it is crucial that you visit the site, talk to our partners and assess the situation yourself. We must also consider a thorough financial and legal audit to verify the robustness of the investment proposals. "

Alex: "I'm going to start by analyzing the market and talking with our local partners. If we can align our goals and establish a solid foundation, I think this expansion could be a great success for us. I insist on ensuring transparency and legality. "

Richard: "Exactly. Keep me updated on your findings and your recommended next steps. This adventure may mark the start of a significant opportunity for our company. "

Alex: "Okay, I'll proceed with caution and diligence. Thank you, dad. I'll keep you posted on my progress. "

Richard: "Exactly. Inform me of your discoveries and your suggested course of action. This adventure may mark the start of something significant for our company. "

Alex "Okay, I will proceed with caution and diligence. Thank you, dad. I'll keep you updated on my progress in Spanish, "he said with an amused air.

Richard: "Perfect. Oh, and before I forget, I'd like you to contact Lukas. He could write a positive article about KARTER Finance. With his journalistic skills and his network, it could really help us strengthen our public image. "

Alex: "Do you want Lukas to write an article about our expansion in South America? "

Richard: "Not just about expansion. I want him to emphasize our financial stability, our expertise in investment management, and our commitment to professional ethics. This would show our partners and potential customers that we are a solid company, led by a strong and visionary leadership. "

Alex: "I see. Lukas excels at finding precise words. His article could really make a difference. "

Richard: "With his help, we can not only promote our expansion but also strengthen our reputation. And don't forget to tell him about our strategy to increase our cash flow. It demonstrates our clear vision and direction. "

Alex: "All right. I'll call him ASAP and explain our plans. His support will be invaluable. "

Richard: "Thank you, Alex. Look, this is more than just an expansion. We have to show everyone that KARTER Finance is irrevocable. Use this opportunity to make our competitors understand that they have every interest in not underestimating us. "

Alex: "I understand. You want us to mark your territory. "

Richard: "My territory is yours too, don't forget it. Your handling of this situation is exemplary. Your ability to see the details while keeping an overview makes you an excellent leader. We must use all our strengths to make this expansion a success. And then, this communication campaign will also be able to wash away the suspicions that have been hanging over you since your public arrest. A positive image of you will strengthen our credibility. "

Alex: "I understand. So, besides promoting the company, I also have to restore my personal image.

Richard: "Right. The business world is ruthless. We must not only be strong, but also appear blameless. That's why I need you at your best, Alex. We need everyone to see what a united and powerful family we are. "

Alex: "I'm going to make sure that we achieve our goals while respecting our values. And I'm going to talk to Lukas. "

Richard: "I don't doubt it for a second. We are continuing this family business together, and I am proud to see how you are taking it to new heights. Never forget that you have all the support of the family and our partners. To stay on top, ruthlessness is necessary, but self-protection is also crucial. "

Alex: "Thank you, dad. I will ensure that I do everything according to the rules and present our company in the best possible way. "

Richard, outstretched arms, grabs Alex's shoulders with his meaty hands

"Alex, one last word, please, you have better things to do. "

Her beloved son leaves the big cubic room and thinks instead of dinner with Tori.

This day overwhelmed him. To understand what I meant this rainy day, it is this inspector who sticks Alex and dissuades him from continuing to be interested in the investigation and his father who supposedly offers him an important opportunity.

Alex had already settled in an intimate corner of the Trattoria Verde, a renowned Italian restaurant. With: Creating a warm and romantic atmosphere, the soft light of the wrought iron candlesticks. The walls, adorned with paintings of Italian landscapes and black and white photos of Rome and Florence, added a touch of authenticity. The bewitching aromas of basil, garlic and fresh tomatoes floated in the air, offering a promise of culinary delights.

Positioned at a tastefully arranged table adorned with a flawless white tablecloth, delicate stemware, and polished silver utensils, Alex was patiently waiting, feeling a touch of nervousness. A bottle of Chianti was lying in an ice bucket next to the table, the shiny ruby wine waiting to be poured. He glanced at his watch, then witnessed Tori entering the restaurant.

Tori entered, attracting all eyes. She wore an elegant dress that hugged her shapes with grace, her hair falling in silky curls over her shoulders. Her eyes shone with a soft, determined glow. As she crossed the room, her heels echoed slightly on the marble floor, adding a touch of sophistication to her look.

She had staked everything to highlight her beauty and her natural charm. Her small suspended handbag rubbed the side of her hip, which made her dress dance in her feminine forms. His blushing face reveals his racing heart, a mix of desire and anticipation fulfilled.

The server greeted her with a professional smile and guided her to the table where Alex was waiting for her. Every step she took seemed imbued with confidence and delicacy, attracting the admiring glances of the other guests.

Alex getting up to greet her Tori: "you look lovely tonight."

Tori all smiling: "Thank you, Alex. This place is really beautiful. Thank you for inviting me here. "

They sat down; the server approaching quickly to open the bottle of Chianti for them. While he was pouring the wine, Alex and Tori exchanged a knowing glance, each appreciating the other's presence in this enchanting setting.

Tori, looking around, admires the setting: "The Trattoria Verde is really a special place. It feels like Italy."

Alex: "Yes, the atmosphere here is amazing. A perfect place to relax and enjoy a good meal after a trying day. We deserve a brief respite. Don't you think so? "

The server brought them the menus, detailing with discreet elegance the specialties of the house. While they were browsing the different dishes, the conversations around them and the soft murmur of Italian music in the background created a soothing and intimate atmosphere.

Tori let a slight smile pass, enough for her beautiful white tooth to reveal her lipstick:

"Alex, I must admit, I've always admired your knack for discovering such delightful places."

The server returned to take their orders, adding a professional touch to the service. As Alex and Tori placed their orders, their eyes met again, each savoring the moment of calm and the connection that settled between them.

Tori: "it was a hard day for all of us for your parents too, I guess. Your presence here is truly helpful. The atmosphere here is soothing, almost magical. "

Alex mentioned: "Oh, you are aware that my dad remains calm in tense situations. Right now it's worse than before. It seems to me that he has the ability to lower the temperature of the Nevada desert. "

Tori reacted by letting out a discreet laugh: "This is indeed the famous Mr. Richard Karter from Greenwood Hills, well tempered like our blacksmiths from our old stables."

The server, dressed with discreet elegance, approached their table and expertly opened the bottle of Chianti. He poured the wine into their glasses with a smile and a few words in Italian before discreetly disappearing.

They ordered their dishes, Alex opting for a tagliatelle Alla bolognese and Tori choosing a risotto ai funghi. While their dishes were being prepared, they continued to discuss; the conversation oscillating between light topics and deeper confidences.

Tori: "Alex, I have always held great admiration for your strength. Even in the most difficult moments, you always seem to keep your calm and your determination. "

Alex "Sometimes you just have to pretend until it gets real. Today, amidst everything that occurred, I truly crave this connection... of this connection. It brings me joy to be with you, Tori. "

With their wine glasses in their hands, they toasted softly, the clink of glasses echoing in the cozy atmosphere of the restaurant. The background violin's soft music added romance.

Tori looking at him intently "I'm here for you, Alex. You can share all the information with me, you understand that. "

Her words held sincerity, yet Alex questioned hidden intentions. The way Tori asked her questions, always with a clear gentleness but a precision that seemed aimed at making him talk more, made him slightly suspicious.

Alex hesitates, saying: "I appreciate you very much, Tori. You are someone special to me. But sometimes I wonder... why now? Why this growing intimacy right after my mother's ceremony? "

Tori seemed slightly unsettled by the question, but she quickly regained her composure.

Tori, Alex, I am cognizant of the fact that the timing may appear unusual, but I have come to the understanding that life is brief and uncertain. I want to save time. I want to help you through this ordeal. You mean a lot to me.

The server returned with their dishes, momentarily interrupting their conversation. The plates, beautifully presented, added a touch of color to their table. Alex took a bite of his tagliatelle, savoring the rich and comforting flavors.

After a moment of silence, "Thank you, Tori. For everything. Your presence really means a lot to me. But I want to be honest. Since the arrest, I have been on my guard. I hope you understand. "

Tori puts her hand on Alex's. "I understand, Alex. I want you to be aware that I'm here for you, without a doubt. I simply desire for you to experience a sense of support and affection. "

Alex gently squeezed Tori's hand, a warmth invading his heart. Perhaps, he thought, he could trust her. For tonight, he leaves his doubts aside and enjoys the moment.

While eating, they continued to chat. The Trattoria Verde offered them a temporary refuge from the worries of the outside world, and Alex found a welcome respite in Tori's company. Other customers' conversations, cutlery clatter, and discreet laughter enhanced the friendly atmosphere.

Tori: "Actually, this place reminds me so much of Italy. I spent a few months there during my studies, and I must say that this restaurant perfectly captures the essence of Italian cuisine and atmosphere. "

Alex: "You in Italy and I in London! "

Tori: "It was our first separation! "

Two friends leave the restaurant, searching for each other, finding a natural game despite their age difference.

Tori dares to invite Alex to have a nightcap at her place, it wasn't midnight yet.

The door closes behind Tori, and an accomplice silence invades the apartment. The soft light of the lamps creates an intimate and warm atmosphere. Alex and Tori are standing there, their eyes immersed in each other, their heartbeats harmonizing.

Tori slowly approaches Alex, her fingers sliding delicately over his arm, drawing invisible lines on his skin. She rises on tiptoe, her shoe with an off-heel, her calves contract to help herself reach what she has long wanted, kisses him, a kiss efflorescing Alex's lips that intensifies. Alex responds to her embrace, her hands sliding down her back, discovering each curve with the infinite tenderness of her V-shaped dress.

They walk together towards the living room, each step a synchronized dance of desire and tenderness. Tori drags her to the couch, where they sit. Still hugging, she takes the initiative. Their clothes become unnecessary barriers that they remove with an almost ritual delicacy.

Alex kisses Tori's neck and over her gold and diamond necklace, her warm lips tracing a kissing path to her shoulder. She closes her eyes, savoring every sensation, every thrill that he awakens in her. His hands explore Alex's athletic torso, pushing back his Egyptian Cotton shirt, enjoying the warmth of his skin under his fingers.

Alex whispers sweet words in Tori's ear, no longer asking for permissions, promises of pleasure and affection. Her hands continue their exploration, discovering the secrets of her body with a precision and a passion that leaves Tori gasping for breath.

Their movements become more intense, a sensual ballet where every gesture is a declaration of love. Alex and Tori get lost in the moment, their minds and their bodies in perfect harmony. Each touch, each kiss, each caress brings them a little closer, uniting them in a communion of passion and tenderness.

Their breaths mingle, skins heat under the intensity of their exchange. Tori feels the desire rising in her, an irrepressible wave of pleasure that overwhelms her. Alex, attentive to every reaction, adapts his gestures, his kisses, responding to his every desire.

Time seems suspended, each second stretched into an eternity of sweetness and pleasure. Together they reach the peak of their passion, a silent cry of shared happiness, an explosion of sensations that leaves them stunned and fulfilled.

While their breathing gradually returns to a normal rhythm, Alex hugs Tori tenderly, their bodies still tangled in contrast with the dim light. They share a knowing smile, savoring the serene perfection. In this intimate cocoon, their love takes a deeper and stronger step.

Tori: "I just offered you Alex. I got naked. It's proof of the trust you."

CHAPTER 4

THE FACES EXPOSED

D ear friends, may our research continue!' Alex takes off his jacket and loosens his tie knot. He pours coffee for all those present gathered around the table extend the billiards. Printed sheets and notes litter the solid wood surface.

Daniel intervenes: "The people who gravitated around Eleanor have interesting profiles,"

While they were dividing up the tasks and rearranging the documents for everyone to read,

Margaret entered the room without announcing herself, a glass of whiskey in her hand in a light silk bathrobe and bare feet appeared of a smaller size. His half-glass weighs his posture forward, strands of hair caress his eyelashes, which do not interfere with addressing the assembly at work in the morning.

"What are you planning now, gentlemen? " She is asking. She has seen the consequences of investigating Alex by this unjust arrest.

"We are working, mom. We are working on it.

Margaret bites the angle of the table to support her seat, lands her glass, extends her arm to support herself: "My son, more stubborn than your father. But much more charming. "

She takes a sip of her whiskey, then continues in a softer voice, "You know Eleanor was wearing on the day of her death a beautiful dress that I gave her from Oscar de la Renta on Madison Avenue in New York for $ 14,000. What a waste of his death, you know! "

"Mom, please, " Alex replies, with contained bitterness.

Margaret heaves a light sigh and stares at her glass. "I'll leave you to your puzzles, and I'll join Jim in the next room. Cheers! "

James WARD called "Jim" Richard's business partner and close to the couple

"My mother to find a new sentence to justify comfort. "

in the frame of the door, Margaret crosses herself with the household staff who brings in the FBI agent Mr. Collins.

"So, say, this mansion is becoming a mill, " she said, laughing. "Hello Mr. FBI agent. Welcome to our humble family home. You're on duty so I'm not offering to share my drink with you. "

"Thank you, Mrs. Karter," Collins keeps his step steady towards Alex. Margaret bows.

Daniel takes his phone out of his jacket pocket.

"Good to see you back with us, Agent Collins," Alex replies.

Alex turns to Daniel: "Let's start with Paul Dawson," he suggests. "He was close to Eleanor and may have noticed something."

Alex nods and dials Paul Dawson's number. A suspicious voice answers quietly after a few tones.

"Paul Dawson on the phone."

"Hello, Mr. Dawson, Alex Karter. I hope you have a few minutes to discuss Eleanor Blackwood."

Paul answers carefully, following a brief silence. "I'm listening to you Alex"

"We have found the disturbing information and think that you may help us."

"I will help if I can. Eleanor was very discreet."

"We understand," Alex said. "The last part of his investigation is what we are trying to piece together. We know the corruption revolved around her. What do you have to say?"

"She mentioned a few names," Paul said after a pause. "People, she suspected. She was never clear with me."

"Do you remember any of these names?" Daniel asks, approaching the other phone to listen.

"She mentioned Councilman Harris and a few others in passing. She was concerned about a man named Victor Dubois. Crossing paths with this person is not advisable. "

Collins continues with the questions, "Mr." Dawson, FBI Agent Collins. What does "this is not someone you should meet" mean?"

"Dubois lacks a good reputation in real estate. I reviewed his questionable sports club investment with the city. Do you remember that? This baseball field, which in fact has become a residence for older adults. He excelled in this field! "

"Thank you, Mr. Dawson," Alex said before hanging up.

Officer Collins, who has been listening to the conversation, intervenes. "It gives us a clear direction. Victor Dubois is a name that often appears in our investigations related to illegal activities for a few years. We have elements, but to date we lack the links between them"

Collins in front of his computer screen illuminating his concentrated face, aside the other faces riveted on the patterns that the agent had established.

As he sifts through another set of financial statements, one name keeps popping up in the documents: James "Jim" Ward, Richard's longtime friend and business partner.

"Jim? "in a voice held by Alex. "Let's be careful. He's with my mother next door. "

Alex realizes the implications. Jim was like family to Alex's father, a trusted figure. That he could be involved in corruption is disturbing.

The friends felt sorry for Alex as he saw names from his father's close circle emerging.

Councilman Harris, Victor Dubois and James Ward.

"I found the name of James Ward and Dubois in our files," Collins says. "If he is involved in this, I should investigate your father, Mr. Karter, soon."

"So let's question Jim" suggests Alex

Agent Collins interjected in a sagacious tone:

"I believe it would be prudent for me to interrogate him, gentlemen." Jim could be more open to talking, knowing that the FBI is questioning him.

'We saw nothing improper about that.'

Alex texts his mother and Jim, inviting them to the mansion's beautiful game room, which has been transformed into a research room for this occasion.

"Mr. Ward, I am the FBI agent continuing the investigation into the death of Mrs. Blackwood and the FBI agent found dead on board her vehicle. "

Jim, 'Hello Sir,'

We interviewed several people and examined a multitude of financial documents. A network of corruption was hovering around Mrs. Eleanor Blackwood.

Jim said, "You are teaching me things, and I am listening to you."

Collins flips through his notes and continues.

"The interrogations showed crucial information. Paul Dawson mentioned Victor Dubois, a name that comes up in suspicious financial transactions. Dubois has strong connections and is associated with influential politicians and financiers in Greenwood Hills. To the FBI, it brings to mind famous FBI cases like the ABSCAM in the 70s, where undercover agents caught politicians red-handed in corruption. "

Jim 'What am I concerned about?'

Collins takes a break,

"The financial schemes that we have discovered are sophisticated. They involve transfers of funds through shell companies, often based in offshore jurisdictions to escape regulatory supervision. These techniques are like those used by criminal organizations to launder money, as with the Italian-American mafia that we dismantled in the early 2000s."

"Mr. Ward, do you have any important elements in the cases that you have handled or pend that could help the FBI in our investigation? "

"My work with Mr. Richard Karter is a business partner. My ties are always professional and our business has always been healthy. If you suspect me, I would be sorry to contact the lawyer whom Alex knows well, by the way. He pulled it out of the "clutches" of your sister Mitchell. "

"I have no further questions Mr WARD. "

Richard's close companion left, shutting the door as he departed. We heard Margaret chatting. The men's silence filled the air with tension, and we couldn't hear anything.

Unsatisfied with contact responses, insufficient to absolve all. Who will bring them satisfaction? Why such opacity in these languages, not easily diluted among family, friends, and even the FBI authority.

"Frustrating! "shouted Daniel. "Only shadows of the world! That we can't make light of it. Does this method suit the corrupt people of the world? "

Lucas asks: "Does luck factor help? "

Alex points out: "Luck is like chance. And chance has no place, or else we risk drifting uncovered. Since these last hours, I impress that we have stirred the troubled bottoms of this city."

"Yet it is a beautiful city, isn't it? "Addressing the agent: "Have you had the chance to discover our pretty park? There is to be lucky. "

Collins: "I drove past in a car. "

Alex is focusing on coffee, which is what I want.

Lucas looks out the window: "Alex, if you'll allow it, I'm going to join your mom and her roses. "

Lucas walks down the porch steps. Margaret finds solace in tending her roses, a peaceful escape from the gardener's duties.

"Margaret, are these your creations?" Lucas asked, pointing at the roses.

Margaret looked up: "Of course, Lucas, my second creation after Alex."

Cabbage and roses! "Alex is nothing like a vegetable! He's been working a lot for the last few days. "

She smiles, putting down her gardening tools and wiping her hands on a cloth: "If you're coming to tell me about Eleanor, let's talk about it. "

"I think she was on something important." Lucas tries to open a confidential conversation.

Margaret's eyes filled with sadness as she sat down on a nearby bench, motioning for Lucas to join her.

"Eleanor was a brave woman. She believed in justice, even when it put her in danger. She mentioned a few names, powerful people whom she was trying to expose and whom she believed to be friends or reliable business partners. But she never gave me any details. "

"Did she ever mention James Ward, Jim? "

Margaret's expression changed: "Yes, she did. Only suspicions and affairs that she had in check with him. It remains personal, you know. To my knowledge, Richard had no problem with Jim,"

Lucas blames himself for his hair: "Do you know what transactions she was referring to? "

"Not specifically. She mentioned that Jim was involved with many "friends ", some of whom were not clean. Eleanor sought solid evidence to protect his investments. "

A moment of silence hung between them, filled only by the rustling of leaves in the gentle breeze. Lucas noticed her eyes filled with pain.

Margaret resumed the conversation. Once, Eleanor mentioned a secret meeting. She was going to confront Jim and a few others about their activities. She believed that if she presented her evidence, she could force them to back down. But she was worried. She knew she was exposing herself to a system.

"Do you know when and where this meeting was supposed to take place? "

"She mentioned it was at the old inn, late at night. She claimed it was the only safe place to confront them and escape city gossip. "

Lucas's mind raced as he processed this new information. The owner reserved the abandoned inn for secret meetings.

Lucas expressed gratitude to Margaret.

Margaret reached out and took Lucas's hand, her grip firm: "Sorry for my attitude earlier, Lucas. I feel like the roses are relaxing me more than the whiskey." Some unsavory people took my best friend's life. Please shed some light.

Puts his index finger on his lips, "You promise me, no crooked article. "

Lucas shaking his hand: "I promise you Margaret, I adore you. "

"The research men," chewing on their cold lunch, saw Lucas back put down his mobile phone, turned on the audio playback of Margaret's recording without his knowledge.

He sat down in the armchair "Listen. "

Alex, "If Eleanor had planned to confront them, they might have realized that she was getting too close and silenced her. "

Collins: "The owner of the plot where the inn is located belongs to Mr. Harris"

Alex: "Another' pain-in-the-ass operation! "

Lucas said: "I like that expression, Alex. Harris bread? I'm kidding, "

Collins: "By listing the properties of Harris and the real estate companies linked to Harris, there is also the real estate real estate company which has taken over investing the Greenwood Hills airfield with an area and not the least of 2 square kilometers, this plot is contiguous to that of the inn. "

Daniel: "What the hell is he to orchestrate these projects? "

Collins: "Marcus hale owner of the land company and guess what gentlemen?! partner of Mr. James WARD our Jim."

Lucas: "Tell me Mr. agent, I'm sure you enjoyed doing puzzles when you were little. "

"But I still do it with my children. "

Alex: "Well, we have the connections! Now Agent Collins, I'll leave the intelligence work on suspicious operations to you Jim/Marcus Hale and Harris/Dubois. "

Their energy devoured all small canapes on the tray for an improvised meal.

The men are busy with their task of speeding up the investigation. Alex from time to time stands aside to manage his time for Karter finance. Daniel and Lucas gather the elements and take notes Collins says from the telephone exchanges of his colleagues specializing in financial banditry, and other calls to other countries. Collins at the head of the table makes a formal outfit worthy of an FBI crisis cell a unique thing of its kind: three civilian contribute to this agent to advance his work, appreciate Alex Karter for his candor and ethics as a financier. The fraternal bond with his former colleague shows Alex's idea of justice and this America of which he cherishes.

Collins stated: "The evidence that we have gathered shows a complex network of corruption and money laundering."

Collins: "Let's start at the top of the pyramid: Sorry Mr Karter it is possible that your father Mr Richard Karter is at the top of the pyramid in the same way as Harris, they are the main beneficiaries of these operations which are based on several shell companies created and managed by his partners."

Alex: "Is Karter Finance affected by this? "

Collins: "Karter Finance is not visible on the organizational chart. "

Lucas: "What types of shell companies does he use?"

Collins: "They use Alpha H Ltd in the Bahamas and Beta Inc. in the Cayman Islands. These entities launder money and hide the illicit origins of the funds."

Daniel asked: "About the workings of these companies and the others on the list."

Collins: "Several shell companies transfer the funds to muddy the waters." For example, the funds go through Gamma Entreprises in Luxembourg, managed by Jim, to Theta Investments in Mauritius, controlled by Marcus Hale."

Alex: "Is it crazy? Jim left the mansion just now? What role does Harris play in this?"

Lucas: "Yes, before your mother started gardening again. "

Collins: "Harris, as an influential politician, uses his power to protect operations. He receives bribes through Delta A Group in Panama and Epsilon Consultants in the British Virgin Islands. In return, he ensures that Richard's projects receive the political support."

Lucas: "We found emails detailing transactions between these entities. These messages reveal the coordination between Harris and Victor Dubois."

Daniel: "So, Victor is preparing the ground, and Marcus Hale is taking over to manage the funds through the shell companies?"

Collins: " Marcus creates and manages the shell companies, ensuring that the funds go through several jurisdictions to evade detection. He works with Jim to coordinate transactions."

Hitting the desk with his fist: "This is all well orchestrated. I now understand my father's urgency to meet the company's board and make an interesting proposal in Panama. "

Collins: "We need financial documents, communications and testimonies. The complex transactions between these shell companies leave traces, and each transfer of funds is a piece of the puzzle. There is also the information that Victor Dubois is an assumed name. Either to protect a wanted person, or to make a dead person forget. "

Daniel wonders if having recordings of the meetings between Victor Dubois, Harris, and Richard in the hostel would provide valuable proof.

Collins: "These recordings are crucial. They show not only the transactions but also the interactions between the key players. This shows their knowledge and active participation in these fraudulent operations."

Alex: "So, what's our next move?"

Collins: " stated that the FBI will investigate Marcus Hale to uncover the true identity of Victor Dubois. Possible cooperation and we will have irrefutable evidence against Harris. We also need to deepen the analysis of financial documents to trace each transfer of funds."

Alex: "Any overwhelming evidence as far as my dad is concerned, too? "

Collins assures Mr. Karter that his father is not a criminal, but rather has connections with the system and questionable individuals. Honestly, he is a suspect.

Lucas: "I guess I can't publish my article yet! my boss is going to make a scene for me'."

Collins: "Every detail counts. We'll dismantle the network and find the murderer of both crimes. "

Alex: "Thank you, Agent Collins. You see yourself being called a crime yourself. What about Detective Mitchell? "

Collins: "An accident does not appear as a savagery. Although we are working in agreement, this remains the FBI investigation. "

Men congratulate each other for their work as a tornado sweeps the table in the games room. Tidy up, as the gentlemen found it this morning. The truth sometimes causes pain for his own father, who might get splashed by the biggest international corruption story. Alex remains in a denial, not yet perceptible. This man, Mr. Richard Karter, builder of an empire starting from a medium-sized city in the USA, would let the fear of having had by his side the worst scoundrel contrary to Alex's values.

Ah, to know if the Spanish language was still in his memory! He remembered this phrase from Richard. Is Richard also a gambler with his own son?

He would not perceive the insult as an ego blow, but rather as a betrayal of honor.

Business, word that only have meaning in those results got by hidden means.

Alex wants to ask these questions to his father during dinner, to investigate and address the family issues that arise during council meetings with Margaret, who supports extravagant therapies and green spaces in affluent neighborhoods worldwide.

Before Richard's return to the manor, Margaret and her son exchange some niceties, Alex ends by instructing him not to talk about the activity they had today.

The little family "coming from a big one" gathered, surrounded by the house staff for dinner while watching before taking place at the press conference of Inspector Mitchell on FOXNEWS. A banal speech out of step with Collins' well-filled file.

The mother and the son remain silent. Richard does not add information to the narrative. Days shorten, but time for gathering plates and glasses filled with childhood's favorite bottled spring water remains unchanged. They said by repeating themselves to confirm that the water is also delicious, which still has the same good taste of yesteryear, fresh and more for summer.

During these moments of family meditation, Alex is searching for the warmth that he longs for in an age where he blames himself for his father. There are thoughts he must put aside. The dizziness deepens when you look from the top of his age. That's what Alex thought during his shared moment with Tori.

Tori, a young lawyer, is in the process of blossoming into a mature woman, leading to love. A magician seeks what he has not found.

A bit of a smile appeared on Alex's face in his thoughts.

"Maybe I need a magician? "He said to himself in his head.

"I thought it would please you, my dears "Margaret cuts the atmosphere too relaxing, or heavy.

"Perfect mom, dad and you?'

"It's always good until the day someone overdoses an ingredient," Richard said with his head down, his meat soaking in the blackcurrant-colored sauce.

"I like it as long as I have the salt at hand. "Margaret replies.

"You seem upset. "Alex sensed a message in this culinary comment from his father.

"Upset to see my son, who thinks he's a detective with his horde of friends! "Richard points the fork in the direction. "Good thing Jim told me the reason for your absence from your office and good luck to you. You are an excellent assistant who follows up and manages appointments. "

"Calm down Richard, Alex does things well, you know; he's a mature man in business too. "

"I saw you have set up an appointment together for tomorrow. Is it something important? "

"The ongoing business for Karter finance is always important Alex. Tomorrow yes"

The dinner seems shorter than usual. This type of exchange was a reminder that Richard is being impulsive. Margaret has this number in mind: Richard swinging the mail angrily in front of him at the entrance. On another occasion, he came close to getting involved in an altercation with a driver who had parked, although his reaction was excessive. His cousin's eyes welled up with humiliation as a man's fist collided with his eye. He screamed, swearing that he was going to call his lawyer.

The patriarch at work, but attaching at first glance a charisma that earned him to win his first contracts at his beginnings.

At the heart of this prosperity of the city stands Karter Finance, an imposing structure of glass and steel, symbol of power and success, with a huge "K" sign dominating the facade. The morning glow illuminates the windows and takes on reflecting the street.

The large hall a prestigious atmosphere. With distinction, the dressed staff embodies the typical profiles of large portfolio managers, exuding splendor. The offices, equipped with the most advanced technologies, a refined furniture chosen by Richard until the paintings he has the last word.

Richard Karter, the patriarch of the company, sitting on the panoramic view. His son, Alex, moved into a nearby office, a sign of the additional responsibilities that fall to him. Their imposing presence creates an atmosphere of tension, each encounter becomes a cockfight.

On the rooftop, an open space cafeteria with a meeting room is a hotspot where senior managers and ambitious young people meet, exchanging ideas and strategies are the scene of lively discussions and crucial decisions.

The activity never falters, whether at the level of complex financial transactions or international expansion strategies. The employees, selected among the best.

Richard has summoned Alex for an important interview. The future of Karter Finance is at stake, and every word, every gesture, could decide it.

"Alex! It's never been the same without you. "

Alex asked: "Are you kidding? I hope so."

Richard: "It's time to stop this charade, Alex. Your little detective game is damaging the company."

Alex: "Harm to the company? Or threatens to reveal truths you prefer to keep buried?"

Richard: "You're not a real investigator, Alex. You are my son, your role is here, don't delve into things beyond you.

Alex: "Maybe I'm not a detective, but I'm able to see the truth."

Richard: "That's absurd. We have customers in South America waiting. Leave this ridiculous investigation and focus on what's important. Every big company has its secrets. What you're doing is only exposing us to unnecessary risks."

Alex: "Unnecessary risks? Like the ones Jim takes to cover for you?"

Richard: "Jim is a loyal partner. He fulfills his duty to safeguard the company. You better learn from him."

Alex, saying nothing, listens to his father and what he learned from the FBI agent. He would have liked to answer him, "Learn from him? Learning to look away when the truth becomes uncomfortable?", but he abstains.

Richard: "Stop playing hero, Alex. It's a cruel world and only the most cunning survive. You won't gain anything by challenging the system."

Alex: "I'm not trying to control everything, just find out the truth. And I won't stop until I find her."

Richard: "The responsibilities you have at Karter Finance are real. You need to put your vigilante fantasies aside and focus on your mission here."

Alex: "My mission here? If your definition of my mission is to ignore your schemes."

Richard: "Do you think you can control everything? That you can understand everything?"

Alex: "I'm not trying to control everything, just find out the truth. And I won't stop until I find her."

Richard: "Do you want to find out the truth? Proceed without company compromise. You're unaware of the opposing forces.

Alex: "Maybe, but I'm willing to take that risk. I will not sacrifice my integrity for your little power games."

Richard: "Drinking a whiskey won't strengthen you, Alex. Look at your mother and go back to the gym to be like your father a warrior's mind. "You need experience and cunning."

Alex: "I don't lack determination. It's something we have in common.

Richard asked, "Do you think you're ready for this?"

Alex: "I've never been so ready. If it means exposing the truth and doing justice, then yes, I am ready for anything."

Richard: "The truth has a price, Alex. A price that you don't seem to understand yet. And this price may well be higher than what you will pay. Keep in mind, once opened, no turning back. And you might discover things you'd rather never have known. However, do not complain when you discover that the world is more complex than you believe."

Alex emphasized that despite the world's grayness, lies should not be accepted.

Richard: "Good luck, in your new office Alex! Since you weren't there, I allowed myself to decide on the decoration. Watch. "

Richard opens a swinging door, his arms throw back the doors on each side.

"Superb". Alex admires his father's skill in bringing the "sheep" back to the "master" with a style that aligns with his own.

Richard, the files on your table are the new ones. Take note. Don't thank me especially, I'm sending you new customers who will increase your interest at the end of the year.

Alex said: "Thanks, Dad. You're making it."

Richard: "And don't bring your friends back and don't attract FBI agents into your paws within our company. Here we only deal with big business, no investigations. "

Alex sees his father swallowing a medical the descent by a large sip of water. And put the little bottle down.

Alex looks surprised: "Are you taking "medoc"? "

"My doctor wishes it, yes, to warn of a risk. You know Alex with our job and my age it's been two."

Alex: "You have a heart of rock, don't worry,"

"It makes me happy, Alex, that you understand what your father wants. I have a smart son. It's like riding a horse for him to advance. Give him a little pat on the flank."

Richard said: "We need fuel today, Alex. And, as Robert De Niro would say, 'I'm fucking hungry as a wolf' before eating his sushi at Nobu."

Richard looks at his watch. "I ordered a special delivery from Nobu for a business lunch between father and son in your new office, worthy of a film producer's lunch! "

While the two senior figures of the city are gorging on a delicious sushi lunch, FBI Agent collins echoes his footsteps on the polished marble of the government building. The security staff greeted him with a respectful nod by letting him pass. Arrived in front of the door of the prosecutor's office, Karen Anderson puts his turned-off phone in his jacket pocket, a brief exchange with the assistant, he opens the door. The prosecutor invites her to sit down while waiting for her to finish her writing.

Agent Collins: "Hello, Mrs. Attorney Anderson. Thank you for receiving me."

Prosecutor Anderson: "Hello, Agent Collins. Your preliminary reports are disturbing. Explain to me the evidence that you have gathered so far."

Agent Collins: "We have uncovered a series of suspicious financial transactions linking several shell companies to Richard Karter. The documents show massive transfers of funds without a clear economic justification. We are investigating these elements, associate the murders of Eleanor Blackwood and former FBI agent, John Farwell."

Prosecutor Anderson: "And these documents, is their authenticity verified?"

"Yes, we have used advanced verification techniques and confirmed the sources of the transactions. In addition, we found encrypted emails between the people mentioned in the file and other key individuals. We are deciphering them."

Prosecutor Anderson: "Perfect. What is your plan for the future?"

Agent Collins: "We must deepen our investigations into the upstream contacts of Richard Karter and Harris. Identifying the people around him and their roles could provide crucial information. In addition, I would like to propose a polygraph test for Richard Karter. Given his central role, this could help us assess the veracity of his statements."

"A polygraph test? This could be tricky. You are aware that Karter's consent is necessary and that the results may not be admissible in court.

Agent Collins: "I understand the implications. However, a polygraph could give us valuable indications about his involvement. Rest assured, we'll ensure compliance."

Prosecutor Anderson: "Very well. Ensure that Karter receives information about his rights and agrees to the test. We can not afford procedural errors, since the drama of Mrs. Blackwood this city is without upside down."

Agent Collins: "I will ensure that we follow all procedures." In addition, we continue to monitor his online activities and his movements. We need warrants to access some of his communication devices.

Prosecutor Anderson said: "I will examine your requests for a warrant." Well, document and justify these measures by examining all the evidence.

Thank you for your support, Madam Prosecutor.

At a critical point, the investigation into the two murders sees the evidence solidifying. The links between several influential figures and illegal financial operations are becoming obvious. The collaboration between FBI Agent Collins and State's attorney Karen Anderson is proving crucial for the next phase of the investigation.

Future actions include targeted interrogations, getting specific warrants, and increased surveillance of suspects. These measures aim to avoid any attempt to manipulate or destroy evidence. Collins, with his experience and determination, understands prizing every detail in this complex case.

Is it sufficient against this murky fabrication by dishonest individuals?

The immediate aim is to strengthen the file with irrefutable evidence before making arrests or searches. Discretion is required, because the slightest leak could compromise months of hard work.

The huge "K" hanging above the entrance symbolizing the power and wealth of the Karter family. Is the scene of strategic decisions that influence the future of many individuals? Wouldn't it risk being too heavy and falling?

CHAPTER 5

SECRETS UNVEILED

The air projected on the face, fluid arm movements, a leg swing that propels the feet forward. Alex oxygenates his blood to boost his energy by going to find his resources deep down. Beads of sweat trickle down his temples, a towel that surrounds his blow, raising his shoulders absorbs a wet neck.

The sun's rays made him squint in certain directions. He holds firm in the face of this discomfort, keeps the course, goes straight ahead.

His well-heated pace gives him confidence to achieve the goal of his cardio.

50 minutes, no pain or cramps is a sign.

He had a good sports ranking in his university at NYU STERN in New York on West Fourth Street. Alex kept all his potential.

A sound signal interrupts him in deep concentration. His mobile phone was telling him he had received a text message. At 6:55 it's a little early. Without stopping, he glances at his message screen from Tori. Curious to read the message in its entirety, he slows down, his muscles congested and hot in a rapid blood flow almost asks him to take a break.

He takes two sips of water, brushes a corner of the towel over his face, dries his eyes to get ready to read.

Message from Tori: "Hello Alex, how are you? I'm coming to the news. Kisses Tori."

She couldn't wait until later in the day to send this text, Alex wonders. An impatience created by her absence linked to Alex's activity. Yet as a lawyer, business is busy days. Tori's thoughts arise and emerge, like this beautiful light this morning.

He does not respond, prefers to wait to finish his physical exercises. He takes advantage of this interruption to stretch and take a good breath. Taking time to answer enhances thinking. A business person in finance must have good reasoning by discarding parasitic emotions.

What's Tori's point? What to understand from this message? Why isn't she on the phone?

The physical recovery is complete. He resumes his journey to the gym where he will spend an icy stream of water before working some parts of his muscular body with machines and free alterations. He buys a few items at the gym shop and eats the protein bar in slow motion, helps assimilation with a recovery drink. Alex's sporting discipline is the opposite of his parents, often associating the athlete's mind with the endurance that it is necessary to handle business.

He poses on this club sofa in duck green velvet.

"Hi Alex, are you okay? Beautiful day! "Exclaims passers-by, sports enthusiasts."

Alex notices other women leave a smile in his eyes between two machines, either for the buttocks or the bust.

The time of the few seconds, he types the answer to Tori.

"I'm fine, I thank you. Currently swamped with work. "

I avoid asking him back to avoid lengthy text messages, as he already helps all day.

Tori brings him back to thinking about his mother Eleanor, too recent for this memory to resurface in the exchanges with Tori. Are Tori's dependencies on Alex driven by the void left by her now-absent parents, who are mentioned in her memoirs - a mother who died in a solvable crime and a father who is considered missing and therefore presumed dead?

This young lawyer saw a very promising start to her career as almost try justice in family law cases, a lack of the father, a duty to understand in the resolution.

Alex saw her more than a psychologist, sharp thoughts who likes to dissect the psychological profile of the client to win a cause. Tori carried the heavy burden of her wealthy family. Since her college, she understood that belonging to high society was not belonging to the entire society.

The comfort comes as with Margaret, whole days of shopping. Friends' meetings were held for those who bought but then forgot their dream purchases, where women from the same world exchanged their 6-month-old crushes. A pretext to drown in the stories of others by valuing themselves that they even everything is fine with their "everything is fine".

Alex abhors redundant futility. His strategy is to find the shortest path quickly for an explanation and receive a suitable answer.

So a short answer came from Tori's message.

Several times, Alex tried and understood what being in a relationship, living it daily, could meet his needs, his desires. But between the fantasy of his parents and Margaret of returning to maternal gestures towards a little son or a little girl did not go in the son's direction, it is not for him a question of fears of founding a home, but his forged a spirit of independent see perfect of solitary who likes to be with himself in front of him.

Fresh and alert to attack his new day, with a solid posture, asserting himself as an athlete who has just won a physical event, he finds his car in his adjusted Italian suit. Alex dominates the dashboard of his Cadillac CT6 car, the tip of his elbow hooked to the door makes him take up all the driving space, his head resting on the seat sewn with black leather a light caresses his hair coming from the sunroof window.

Even with electronic modes, the Cadillac remembered the destination it sought for its beloved elegance and performance. When he gained a new car, his choice fell on a Cadillac, an iconic model of sophistication and power. The comfort of the road made him recall this memory during his visit to Empire Cadillac in Long Island City. The sales representative welcomed him. She made him discover every detail of the vehicle with an obvious passion and expertise.

"You have chosen a vehicle that integrates technology, comfort and performance, Mr. Karter," she explained to him. "By following the principles of a fluid purchasing journey, the welcoming Empire Cadillac team and our showroom enhance the exclusivity of the experience."

These words struck Alex as he sat behind the wheel for the first time. Feeling luxury and mastery that he felt confirmed his choice. Crossing the streets of New York with ease to the mansion, he knew he had found a partner who lived up to his ambitions.

As Alex says, the first best value is the right advice.

"Hello Mr. Karter, good day Sir' The daily standard phrase that the parking security officer says every time the Karters come.

Alex answers him every time. His father is something else ... sometimes.

Dress casually at Alex these days, no ties needed. Some wear sportswear during sunrise, while others dress down a few hours before the weekend starts. He cultivates a charisma that is dear to his heart and wears beautiful handcrafted products. Meaning lies in generations passing down know-how.

In the elevator, a selfie photo of his Italian suit, just a photo for a message intended for Tori.

"The Italian know-how;"

Tori's answer will come soon.

' ☺ '

Adult seduction game for mutual desire.

Before the elevator doors open, he hears the loud voice of a man shouting incomprehensible yet angry phrases.

With a hurried step, Alex understood his father was in a state of hysteria. Before entering his closed office, the assistant jumps on him from her chair,

"It's your father, Mr. Karter," she said in an embarrassed voice

"Tell me, what is happening to him so early in the morning? " Alex worried.

"Your father is on the phone with his lawyer. This concerns the ongoing investigation," he said, adjusting his tunic and walking close to the trendy shops.

"Avoid taking incoming phone calls while he calms down. "

"Good Mr. Karter" she sits down and pings on the keyboard of her computer.

Alex wonders if maturity is not just a matter of age. To hear his father screaming in anger at Karter finance is for him an example to follow. No matter what angers him, the patriarch's day started and will continue well. Introduces these wireless headphones into his ears, push them in with his thumb, turns up the sound of one of his favorite music in front of the screams of the office neighbor that a distant noise like a neighborhood dog known for often opening its mouth becomes lessened.

Richard asked condescendingly: "What is this lie test request?" They think they can drag me through the mud like that?

The Lawyer: "Richard, calm down. It's just a tactic to destabilize you. They have nothing solid against you.'

"Do you want me to calm down?! Do you realize what this entails? If I refuse, they will say that I have something to hide! "

"I understand your frustration, Richard, but there are ways to challenge this request. The lie test is not mandatory in criminal investigations, except in very specific circumstances. "

Richard squeezes his point hard.: "There's no way I'm letting these fuckers get my name dirty! What do you propose, then? "

"We're going to put together a solid case to show that this request is unjustified. We can invoke the right to silence and non-self-incrimination, protected by the Fifth Amendment. Furthermore, courts often deem lie detector results as unreliable and inadmissible. "

"However, I want it to be done." Every minute wasted, it's one more minute for them to go through my stuff.

"I'll take care of it. In the meantime, avoid telling anyone about this case, even Alex. The less he knows, the better for us.'

Richard with a sarcastic air: "Yes, because my son could become a mole, right? Don't worry about Alex, he's smart. But I want to see results. "

"Understood, Richard. I'll call you back as soon as I hear. "

Richard hangs up, throws his phone surfing on the table.

He utters one last word out of his mouth, "And shit!".

Prosecutor Anderson: "Agent Collins, what's the latest on Marcus Hale and Victor Dubois? "

"Prosecutor Anderson, we found out that Marcus Hale died a year ago in Florida. The circumstances of his death are suspicious, which had led to opening a homicide investigation by our Florida State FBI office. "

Prosecutor Anderson: 'Suspicious? In what?'

"Hale was in good health. There are inconsistencies in the medical reports and clues left at the scene that suggest that criminal means have caused his death. "

Prosecutor Anderson: 'Do you have any concrete evidence that supports this hypothesis?'

"Yes. Financial transactions show significant money movements between the accounts of Hale and Dubois. These transactions suggest Hale played a central role in the fraudulent network we are investigating. "

The prosecutor leaned forward, eyes focused and ears tuned in. "Tell me about these transactions," they demanded.

Agent Collins opens a file in front of him:

"Hale was in regular contact with Dubois until his death. We found encrypted emails and phone records that show that they were in constant communication. In addition, the amounts moved between their accounts are considerable and correspond to money laundering schemes. Hale was also involved in small money laundering transactions through commercial real estate transactions, including spas, beauty salons, and other small businesses. "

"And what about Victor Dubois? "

"Dubois is nowhere to be found. We believe that this is a code name used to hide the real identity of a network member. We believe that "Dubois" is a code name used to hide the real identity of a network member. "

"Any idea who could be hiding behind this fake name? "

"Not yet. But Dubois is playing a link in the chain. We must continue to monitor financial transactions and communications to find out. "

"What are the next steps, Agent Collins? "

"We have to question the prime suspects, starting with Richard Karter, under a lie detector if possible, but we had a refusal from his lawyer. It could also give us an idea of his reactions under pressure. "

The Prosecutor with a wry smile: "Richard Karter and Harris... He seems to like Florida, doesn't he? Maybe he often goes there for a vacation. It would be unfortunate if he had to prolong his stay for other reasons. "

Agent Collins: "Indeed, prosecutor. We will clarify his movements and activities in Florida. "

"Very well. I'm going to approve the request for the lie detector interrogation," said the person in authority. They emphasized prizing covering all legal bases and gathering solid evidence before making any arrest or search.

"Got it, prosecutor. We will try to strengthen our case. "

"Keep me informed of each development. The murderer walking doesn't reassure me. Two murders in a short time. "

"Something else." Collins documented the additional forensic expertise that the team had conducted on Agent Farwell. He gathered his questions from memory.

"We have completed the forensic analysis regarding Farrell's neck injury, and the results are concerning.

Farrell's injury does not correspond to a classic car accident. Typical lesions, such as whiplash or vertebral fractures, are absent. Instead, we discovered an atlanto-axoidal dislocation. These signs suggest an intentional twisting of the nape. "

The prosecutor frowning: "An intentional twist? Do you mean someone attacked him? "

"In car accidents, drivers often experience whiplash due to sudden head movements. This leads to injuries such as cervical sprains or vertebral fractures. Look at the report. The imaging reveals Farrell's injuries: an atlanto-axoidal dislocation with an extreme lateral inclination, showing that someone turned his head in an unnatural direction."

The Prosecutor is trying to understand the purpose of Collins' idea "So, someone would have grabbed his head and turned it? "

That is what the evidence suggests. The evidence suggests that the force required to cause such an injury far exceeds what one would expect from a car accident. It looks more like a violent assault. It is possible that someone attacked Farrell before or after the accident, or that someone staged the accident to mask a homicide.

"This complicates things even more, Agent Collins. Who could be behind all this? "

"This discovery suggests that someone wanted to silence Farrell and prevent him from investigating. Someone was aware of Agent Farwell's recent takeover of the investigation in "Off" by Mr. Alex Karter. "

Prosecutor, concentrate on close associates and potential motives: "You mentioned a certain Jim. "

Agent Collins: "This is a lead to explore. "

'Thank you for your work, Agent Collins. We possess inadequate evidence for charges, but enough for your investigation's direction."

At the wheel of his car, Agent Collins on his way back to his office dials Lucas's number.

"Lucas, this is Agent Collins from the FBI. Come to the office immediately. I have a proposal that could help us move the investigation forward. "

Collins appointment is taken by Lucas, and he says: "I'll be right there." His priority is to make it.

On his computer keyboard, he sticks a post-it note that says, "I'll be back in an interview." Exiting his partitioned journalist's office, he takes a few steps towards the parking lot of the local newspaper building, gets into his car, and starts driving at high speed. His car is his second desk, notes, papers of all kinds, a cup of coffee not finished from the previous day. He activates his window cleaner and windshield wipers to get better visibility of the road. Its press sticker stands out better. While driving, he notices the mess in the passenger seat, finds a public trash can, stops to throw the biggest unimportant one there.

Lucas crosses the controls that allow access to Collins' office. Wait until Collins picks him up.

A corner of the waiting room made for guests, a coffee machine, a fresh water dispenser. In the meantime, he straightens up to treat himself to a cappuccino while he takes care of himself.

After a good quarter of an hour, he hears footsteps echoing in the corridor, maybe it's him, he says to himself, pushing into an angle while finishing drinking the foam.

Collins appears at the right angle in his navy blue suit. "Thank you for coming, Lucas. "

The two men walk along this corridor, which leads to some open doors. A woman in uniform crosses them.

I have an idea, but I need your help as a journalist.

"What do you have in mind, Collins? "

He opens his office door to let Lucas pass in front of him,

"Please take a seat. I will explain to you the reason I brought you here today. "

We know that some of our suspects are hiding behind aliases and shell companies. If we publish a strategic article, we could encourage them to make mistakes. Have you ever used your pen for this kind of maneuver?

"Yes, I've done that a few times. Publish information to put pressure on the suspects. Please be both precise and credible. What kind of article are you considering?

Collins shared his idea with Lucas

"I was thinking about something that reveals the links between Marcus Hale, who is now confirmed dead, who was part of the quartet of launderers, that's what I call them, and their money laundering operations. We suggest we have more information than we have to make them panic. "

"I like that. " Answer Lucas by repositioning themselves on his chair in front of the desk.

"It could push them to communicate with each other or make careless movements. But I'm going to need precise and convincing details. And my editor needs to be informed. She's already pressing me for a big scoop. "

The agent hands the documents 'Here's what we have so far. Marcus Hale was involved in suspicious transactions related to beauty salons, spas and other small businesses. We know he died a year ago in Florida under suspicious circumstances. If we can insinuate we have solid evidence, that should be enough.

In his letter, Lucas makes a proposal,

'We are going to publish an article implying that Marcus Hale was about to reveal the money laundering operations before his suspicious death in

Florida.' We must also mention the quartet of launderers on Greenwood Hills without mentioning specific names.

"Perfect. We clarify this quartet is under pressure and could make mistakes. This should push them to make careless movements.

Already, Mr. Richard Karter and his lawyer oppose lie detectors, and he became angry when he learned that.

Lucas said: "I'm also going to include an anonymous quote from a 'source close to the investigation' stating that search warrants are imminent." This should make them sweat. What do you think about it?'

"Great idea. They must sense the tightening net. Make sure your editor agrees with this approach."

Lucas expresses doubt, asking: "What if someone discovers that we are manipulating information?"

"We're just doing our job. Sometimes you have to play hard to get results. If this pushes them to make mistakes, we'll have evidence to present. "

"Thank you, Lucas. We need to get them out of their burrows. "

The secret conversation ends with a good handshake, sealing an agreement in silence.

Lucas, more than motivated, leaves the place with renewed determination. His boiling mind is already considering the headlines he could create. He gets into his car, the engine purring as he drives down the road, leaving the city for a temporary destination. The landscapes pass before his eyes, but his mind remains fixed on the upcoming revelations and the impact of his future article.

After a few minutes of driving, he feels hungry. Spotting a typical retro American diner by the side of the road, he stops for a burger. The luminous sign, an old flashing neon sign, promises good food and a moment of respite. The diner is a real throwback to the 50s, with its red leather benches, individual jukeboxes on each table, and its walls adorned with photos of rock stars and old American cars.

As he enters, the tantalizing smell of grilled meats and French fries invades his nostrils, offering a welcome break from his intense reflections. The bell hanging on the door tinkles, attracting attending a middle-aged server with a tired but sincere smile. Behind the counter, a server in retro uniform with a ruffled apron is busy, bringing plates loaded with food to relax-looking customers.

Lucas sits, orders a burger, and engages the server, a man with graying hair and a benevolent look.

"Nice day for a long drive, huh?" the server begins, wiping a cup of coffee with a red and white checkered tea towel.

"Yes" Lucas replies, appreciating the simplicity of the exchange. "I'm from Greenwood Hills, do you know?"

The server nods: "Oh, yes. Many people are talking about this city. Rumors, stories... Are you there for work?"

Lucas smiles, a glimmer of secrecy in his eyes: "We can say that. I'm a journalist'.

The server raises an eyebrow, intrigued: "Interesting. You must have interesting stories to tell."

"This one could be crucial," Lucas says as he gets his burger. The brioche bread, browned, contains a juicy meat topped with melted cheese, fresh tomatoes and crunchy lettuce. He takes a first bite, enjoying the rich and comforting flavor.

The server walks behind the counter, fills her glass with soda with a smile and continues her service, leaving Lucas to enjoy his meal. The dinner, with its retro atmosphere and soft rock music in the background, offers a welcome parenthesis, a moment of calm before the media storm it is about to unleash.

As he finishes his burger, Lucas takes out his notebook and scribbles down some ideas, tweaking the title of his article: "The quartet of launderers from Greenwood Hills: laundering and murders." He knows these words will attract attention and provoke powerful reactions.

Once his meal is over, he thanks the server and the server, leaves a generous tip, and goes back on the road. His sharpened mind is ready to write the article that could change Greenwood Hills.

Meanwhile, during this general lunch break, the shops become active.

Beautiful slender legs mounted with heeled shoes come out of a boutique, the embossed white bags of the luxury brand rub on the upper thigh. Its raw milk-colored skirt suit gives a neutrality of elegance.

The heels slam the stone slab floor, a rectilinear step that juxtaposes on the front of his feet.

Tori has just splurged, and her adrenaline motivates her to call Alex.

Alex, under a pile of files at work, picks up the phone while his computer remains frozen.

"Hey Alex, I treated myself a bit. Can we grab lunch sometime? "

"So your second madness would be a lunch with me?"Alex he says

"Listen Alex, I'm a stone's throw from Grill & Co, will you join me? "

"It's noted Tori, by the time I get there I'm ordering something. "

174

With small steps in a hurry, it makes you reason even more like the sharp clattering of hooves.

The tables at Grill & co are all busy, the success of the restaurant has been felt since the takeover of a well-known chef who has left Vegas for a few years, the best dishes of the day with fresh products, every day the menu dish always highlighted with surprising creativity that causes the interest of connoisseurs and accustomed to good tables. In the evening, a cocktail brunch place brings together young couples in love in a warm atmosphere.

Tori with a raised finger sign like a shy student to ask for something pushed up by her toes. A strap of her pump dropped from the heel. She calls:

"Please! "

The server approaches her carrying a large diameter tray like a giant disc, a few plates.

"Hello Madam, how many does the lunch cover?"

"Hello, for two, please. "

The server scans both the room and the terrace. There would be a 15-minute wait,

'I suggest you go to the bar in the meantime.'

'Well, you're kind.'

Tori takes her ease loaded with her bags while consulting the map. She did not go unnoticed, sitting on a bar chair on a metal leg crossed legs and her always exaggerated arch gives her the air of a wasp waist ready to take out his dart of seduction on the surrounding men. Place the card down, click her bag, dip her fingers to retrieve the accessory for Alex's staging.

Tori's dopamine is at its peak when she notices Alex entering the restaurant, accompanied by a server who prepares their table.

Tori says: "Alex," as he dangles his hands free.

"My Alex, delighted that you could respond to my invitation, a little unexpected, isn't it?!"

"It's Tori, no comment" By pouting confirms that Tori's character no longer has any surprises for him.

The couple, without being it settles around the round table enlisted with an edge of a golden metal. The glossy black surface gives way to plates, glasses and napkins folded origami-style.

What is this invitation worth, Tori? We subscribe to excellent restaurants.

"A desire to see you again already, and look at Alex, a crazy blow. "

She unfurls a dress in front of her, so short that it looked like a top.

"So," she said, eager to know his opinion.

'This outfit must fit you, mmm, very sexy. "

"Yes, Alex, I think so too. I want to be feminine. "

Even without that desirable new dress, Tori, you know it well.

"Alex, you're nice to me..."

"Let's order. I'm starving! "

A quick decision makes up for the previous expectation.

Tori takes off her double-breasted jacket, settles it on the chair. A pretty silk blouse hanging from her shoulders by thin chain straps.

Alex felt a well-determined hidden game of seduction, but for what?

Tori starts questioning from the first drink and fork strokes.

"How is business? "

"Well, even very well. Despite the ongoing criminal cases by the FBI, the company is expanding rapidly. "

"Is the FBI taking over the investigations?"

Since the death of one of their retired agents, the FBI has been concerned.

A break from Tori,

"I see. What about Richard?"

"My father is solid as a rock. He has enough reserve for his outbursts of anger. "

Compassionate Tori: "I understand well, you know, my father also had a strong character. "

"Do you talk about your father? Is it the pain that prevents you from expressing? "

"The pain of having learned from Italy that my father was missing, it's hard to accept that so young, "

Alex listens to Tori's words, wipes her lips with the help of the beautiful cotton towel, takes a break, analyzes the emotional sentences expressed by this beautiful young single woman.

He did not understand why Tori, in her most beautiful period of her age, remains single. Is it this family trauma?

"In fact, the reason I offered you lunch today is that I just got back from my notary's office about my mother's inheritance, and it is that despite heavy debts of which I had no knowledge. Mom leaves me a generous inheritance. "

"Happy for you Tori, well use it, " Alex retorts with a distant air

"I want us to spend more time together. I understand your work consumes your time, but I hope it doesn't consume your entire life."

Alex felt annoyed because she wasn't getting to the point of her idea.

"I'm listening to you Tori. "

"That's it." I'd like us to travel somewhere. What do you think? She tilts her face, her velvet cat eyes pleading for an answer that she desires.

"A great idea. It's a question of organization. My father is sending me on a business trip to Panama. We don't have a date. "

Tori arches over, smiling at the corners of the corners,

"Good news for you Alex! you can make a small space for me in your suitcase. "

"Not the type to hide a beautiful woman's body in a suitcase! " His sarcastic humor appeals to women and to himself by the sense of derision.

Tori swallows with her throat clenched. Expressionless face.

"A dessert" she says? "I've already chosen. You know, Grill & Co makes the best vanilla souffles with their ginger chocolate shavings. "

"No thanks Tori, not for me. "

180

"So let me ask for two spoons," Tori winks at him.

He felt Tori was pulling out her great seduction game. He takes her as the intermission of the day.

She resumes her role as a desirable woman like that famous evening in the Italian restaurant. Alex thinks she won't dare after this lunch to make love to him...

At the end of the meal, Tori settles for lunch when she goes to the bathroom.

Just like her, he feels immense gratitude for this delectable act of sharing.

With a stolen kiss, she kisses him on a corner between his cheek and his blow.

Here is the young Tori Blackwood becomes a millionaire in a short time after the murder of her mother, knowing that she knows it will be necessary to "pay off" the unforeseen debts.

Collins, accompanied by his faithful collaborator Agent Taylor, is preparing for a series of decisive actions for the investigation, with the approval of the Prosecutor. Their first step is to check the movements of James Ward known as "Jim" in Florida last year. Taylor contacts the airlines to get flight records, while Collins deals with car rental agencies and hotels to get additional information. Once they confirm the travel data, they turn to communications analysis and collaborate with an electronic surveillance technician to review Ward's phone records and emails. Their goal is to discover suspicious calls and messages from Florida during the key period.

With permitting, the Prosecutor, Collins and Taylor use advanced FBI techniques to conduct their investigation.

They are reviewing police and autopsy reports regarding the death of Marcus Hale, seeking to identify any potential links. By working with local authorities in Florida, they hope to get additional testimony and evidence, including interviewing potential witnesses and monitoring concordant interactions. The in-depth analysis of the financial transactions between Ward and Hale completes their investigation, allowing them to discover unusual or suspicious movements of funds.

At the FBI office, Collins and Agent Taylor are poring over a stack of documents and computer screens.

"Taylor, we need to confirm James Ward's whereabouts in Florida last year. Let's start with the flights. "

"I'll take care of it. I will contact the airlines and check the car rental agencies. "

"Perfect. Meanwhile, I'll investigate hotel registries for insights. "

The agents keep in touch with the representative of the airline.

"Hello Sir, how can I help you today? "

"We are investigating an individual named James Ward. Could you check if he took flights to Florida last year? "

"Of course. Give me a moment to access the recordings. "

The representative consults his computer

"There you go. James Ward took a flight to Miami in March. "

'Thank you. This matches our criteria. "

They follow up with the contact of the representative of the car rental agency.

"CarsUGo rental agency, Hello "

Brief presentation of the agent.

"We are looking for information on car rentals made by a certain James Ward, last year in Florida. "

"I'll check that out right away. "

"Yes, Mr. James Ward rent a car in Miami in March. "

"Thank you for your cooperation. "

Comes the turn of hotel establishments in Florida.

"Hello, we are investigating a certain James Ward. Do you have any recordings of his stay here last year? "

"I remember him. He stayed here in March. He requested a room overlooking the sea. "

Collins and the FBI's electronic surveillance technician are reviewing the phone records.

"Here are James Ward's phone records for last year. We see several calls and messages coming from Florida in March. "

"Excellent work. This confirms our suspicions. Let's continue to monitor his communications for any other relevant information."

Agent Taylor: "We confirmed that James Ward was in Florida in March of last year. His movements coincide with the period of Marcus' death. "

Collins and Agent Taylor are sitting at a table reviewing Marcus Hale's forensic report.

"Look at this, Taylor. The forensic report shows that Marcus Hale died of a broken neck. Describing the injury is very accurate. "

"A broken neck..." wonders Taylor. "They mention that the lesion is consistent with a violent blow inflicted by a third person." It appears deliberate, not accidental.

Cervical fractures occur from deliberate and targeted force. It's the same type of injury as Farrell's, remember?'

"Yes, Farrell also had a cervical fracture. The report mentioned a violent head rotation, resulting in a cervical vertebrae rupture. This is a rare injury, requiring considerable strength and precise technique. "

'That's it Taylor. The medical examiner emphasizes that the impact requires considerable force and that the angle shows aggression rather than a fall. This similarity is disturbing.'

"So we're talking about an attacker who knows what he's doing. We're talking about an attacker who has expert knowledge of human anatomy and knows how to inflict this type of trauma. "

"A real professional or someone with a specific training. And that brings us back to Jim. His movements coincide with the period of Hale's death. We need to dig deeper into this lead. "

"Does the report mention any signs of wrestling or other defensive injuries? " Taylor wonders.

Collins analyzes the elements of the report.

"Just a few bruises on the arms and wrists, typical of someone trying to defend themselves. But nothing sufficient to suggest a prolonged struggle. It's as surprise has taken it. "

"It corresponds to a fast and effective attack, as for Farrell. We could be exist a specific modus operandi, right, Collins? "

"We need to dig deeper into this lead. Perhaps Jim has some skills or background that could explain this ability. We also need to check if there are any links between the victims, apart from Jim. "

Taylor is a specialist in money laundering and trafficking. What if it is associated with settling accounts? Hale could have had debts or unpaid amounts of money. Jim could be involved.

"It's a plausible hypothesis. If Hale owed money to someone influential, execute this type could serve as a warning. We need to examine Hale's finances to see if there are any suspicious transactions or unpaid debts. Jim could be a collateral victim or even an intermediary. "

"I'm going to check Jim's work history and see if he has any combat training or similar skills. Then I'll move on to Hale's finances to check for anomalies. " Concluded Taylor.

Collins, who is investigating diligently, 'In the meantime, I will review the other unsolved cases with similar injuries. Discovering similar fractures in other victims could lead us to the attacker or a larger network.

"Are you thinking of something specific? "

"Mrs. Blackwood. Mrs. Blackwood's file states that she fell down the stairs, but the medical examiner observed that her neck was broken before the fall. It could be the same attacker. "

"Interesting Collins. Maybe we should reconsider his case with this new perspective. If we can prove that the same person is responsible, we'll have a solid lead. "

Collins picks up his phone right away to contact the Prosecutor.

"Hello, Collins. I received your report on the Marcus Hale case. Can you tell me more about the new data you have collected? "

"Of course, Mr. Prosecutor. We have confirmed that Marcus Hale died of a broken neck caused by a violent blow, consistent with an assault. This type of injury is like those suffered by Farrell and Mrs. Blackwood. For the latter, we now believe that someone broke her neck before she fell down the stairs. "

"Interesting. You mentioned suspicious movements of James Ward in Florida. Can you expand? "

From the flight and car rental records, it is evident that Ward was in Florida in March last year, precisely around the time Marcus Hale was killed. In addition, his phone records show several calls and messages from Florida during this period."

"So, you think Ward is involved? "

Uncertain, but the disturbing coincidences are noticeable. It is possible that Ward is involved or that he has crucial information. We also suspect settling accounts related to debts or unpaid sums of money.

"I see. So you're asking for a wiretap and electronic and physical surveillance of Ward? "

"We believe these steps will allow us to gather additional evidence and understand Ward's role in this case. We need to identify his contacts and activities in order to progress with our investigation."

"I understand prizing these measures. Do you already have any elements that could justify this request before a judge?'

"We have in our possession the flight records, the telephone records, the forensic reports and the disturbing similarities between the cases of Hale, Farrell and Mrs Blackwood. All these elements show a pattern that deserves a thorough investigation."

"I will approve your request. Ensure you follow the proper legal procedures for obtaining permissions. We must be blameless on this point."

"I thank you, Mr. Prosecutor. We will proceed and we will keep you informed of any significant progress."

"Do this. Good luck, Collins."

The mantle of leadership, inspired by the example they had set. The story of their fight for justice and the legacy of Eleanor Blackwood became a part of (Greenwood)'s lore, a reminder of the power of courage, determination, and unity.

One evening, as the sun set over (Greenwood), casting a golden glow across the town, Alex stood on his porch, reflecting on the journey that had brought them to this moment. He felt a profound sense of gratitude for the friends and community that had stood by him through thick and thin.

Lucas and Daniel joined him, and together, they watched the sun dip below the horizon, signaling the end of one chapter and the beginning of another. They knew that the future would bring new challenges, but they also knew that they were ready to face them, united in their commitment to justice and integrity.

As the first stars appeared in the night sky, Alex turned to his friends, his voice filled with determination and hope. "The journey continues, but we've shown that together, we can overcome anything. (Greenwood) is our home, and we'll protect it with everything we've got."

Lucas and Daniel nodded in agreement, their hearts full of the same resolve. "To the future, " Lucas said, raising an imaginary glass. "And to the legacy we're building every day. "

"To the future, " Alex and Daniel echoed, their voices strong and unwavering.

And so, with the support of their friends and the community, they stepped forward into the future, ready to face whatever challenges lay ahead, knowing that they had the strength and unity to build a better tomorrow for (Greenwood).

CHAPTER 6

WHEN HILLS FALL

An opulent residential area of recent construction, the alleys almost deserted at this time of day. The houses, all similar, are distinguished only by a few details, with the exception of one, in front of which two luxury cars are parked. Other cars, a little further away, lined up on the same roadway, testify to an unusual activity.

The soft afternoon light penetrates into a room of this house. Scattered clothes and lingerie litter the carpet, a pair of stilettos abandoned further away. Two naked bodies, partially covered by a sheet, reveal a woman's leg raised and a man's hand clasping her ankle. Jim and Margaret are lying in bed, enjoying a moment of relaxation.

Margaret whispers in Jim's ear: "Jim, would you like some coffee? I'll make some."

"Yes, thank you. Just a cup, I have a meeting with you know who."

"No, I don't see," Margaret replies with an amused tone. "Ah, are you talking about that rich man from Greenwood Hills?"

"Exactly, my pretty one. The most troublesome man in business."

Margaret and Jim get up. Margaret puts on her stockings and dives into her trouser tunic, while Jim, with a quick gesture, buckles his belt. Coffee in hand, Jim checks his phone while Margaret struggles to get up and running.

"My legs are cut off, Jim. I wish we could put this back on and open a good bottle from your cellar."

Suddenly, a series of powerful knocks sounded at the front door, breaking the tranquility of the moment. Curious neighbors begin to look out of their windows at the cars in line blocking the front of the house. Disturbed by this interruption, Margaret and Jim exchange worried glances.

"Who can be there at this hour, Jim?"

Jim peeks out the window and sees black cars.

He walks to the door, glancing quickly through the window to catch a glimpse of three FBI agents in official attire. Their serious and determined expressions do not portend anything good.

"Agent Collins," one of them said, showing his FBI badge. "We have an arrest warrant for James Ward."

Jim opens the door, jaw clenched. "For what reason?"He asks.

"Mr. Ward, you are under arrest on suspicion of fraud and obstruction of justice."Collins dictates his rights.

Margaret, trying to interpose, her voice trembling, said: "Wait, there must be a mistake. Jim didn't do anything wrong!"

Agent Taylor, calm but inflexible, and surprised to see Mrs. Karter at Jim's house, replies: "Mrs. Karter, please step aside. We have strong evidence and a legal warrant."

"It's ridiculous. I'm innocent. You must have the wrong person."

FBI agents follow strict protocol. Officer Collins approaches Jim, asks him to turn his back and cross his hands. He puts the handcuffs on her, squeezing slightly to make sure they fit snugly. Agent Taylor is keeping Margaret at bay.

"Jim! Don't let them do that! Tell them you didn't do anything!"

"I'm going to prove my innocence, I'm going to call my lawyer. Don't worry, Margaret."

"You are going to be taken for a lie detector test. Any resistance will only aggravate your situation."

Jim, with his wrists shackled, is taken to the exit by the FBI agents. Margaret, her eyes misty with tears, looks at them, helplessly. Neighbors whisper to each other, some taking photos or videos with their phones.

Margaret stays in her car for a while, her arms resting on the steering wheel, devastated. The cars start, driving away from the residential area, leaving Margaret alone and distraught. The last agent checks the house one last time before leaving.

Lucas's explosive article in the Greenwood Hills Journal had the effect of a bomb. Revelations about money laundering operations and the names of some people involved were making waves on social networks. Detective Mitchell, in particular, was furious. How could this journalist have obtained information that even the local police had not yet obtained? Had Lucas accessed sources unknown to everyone? Decided to get her hands on the elements developed in the article that Lucas must have possessed.

Harris, imposing but of medium height, floating in his suit to hide his curves, kept the newspaper on the page of Lucas's article. Two fingers held a cigar in the other hand, while he grabbed the phone.

"It's Harris!", he shouted. "What the hell is this, Mitchell? Have you read this article? How could this journalist have obtained this information?"

Sitting at her desk, rereading Lucas's article, Inspector Mitchell no longer hid her annoyance and frustration. "I read the article. We will investigate to find out how he got this information."

"Take him into custody! I want to know who spoke to him. This information was not to come out."Harris, enraged, continued, "Decidedly, you are not showing your motivation for the help I am giving you for your promotion."

"I assure you, Harris, the city police department has just been mobilized for the arrest of Lucas."

At the newspaper, the sirens of the police cars mark a time out for their activity. This is the first time that an entire police patrol has arrived at the foot of the building. A volume of uniformed police officers invests the place as if to search for a criminal or a group of wanted gangsters.

"Lucas Bennett, you are under arrest for concealing evidence."

Lucas, stunned, stands up slowly, raising his hands in a sign of surrender. "What? You can't do that! I simply followed a journalistic lead."

Detective Mitchell: "You have in your possession crucial evidence for our investigation. You deliberately hid them. It's a crime, Lucas."

Lucas' Editorial Chief: "Wait, Detective Mitchell, Lucas has only done his job. He didn't do anything wrong."

"I acted as a journalist! My duty is to discover the truth and expose it. Everything I found is in the article."

Detective Mitchell: "Don't play smart with me. We are going to find out the whole truth, and if you lied or omitted information, you will suffer the consequences."

The police hand Lucas the handcuffs under the shocked and disapproving gaze of his colleagues. Whispers spread in the editorial office.

"You can't take her away like that!"

Detective Mitchell: "We'll see."

The police officers take Lucas out of the editorial office. His colleagues, still in shock, whisper and exchange worried glances.

Outside, Jim's neighbors are buzzing. The images of Jim's arrest, captured on their phones, are already circulating on social networks. Short videos show Jim in handcuffs, escorted by FBI agents, while murmurs spread among the spectators. But one detail especially attracts the attention of the spectators: among the agents and Jim, a well-known figure clearly stands out. Margaret Karter, her elegant posture but her marked face and her tousled hairstyle, is visible on several shots and videos, triggering a wave of speculation and rumors.

Jim is sitting in an interrogation room at the FBI office, his hands cuffed on the table. The cold neon light illuminates the room, accentuating the oppressive atmosphere. He waits, anxiously, glancing nervously at the clock above the door.

The door opens, and two lawyers enter, their assured gait contrasting with Jim's palpable anxiety.

Callahan: "Mr. Ward, I'm Richard Callahan, and this is my colleague, Samantha Blake. We are here to represent you."

Jim: "Thank you for coming so quickly. They want me to take a lie detector test. It's senseless, I'm innocent!"

Blake: "Don't worry, Jim. We will do everything to prevent this test. Lie detectors are notoriously unreliable and often inadmissible as evidence."

The FBI agents then enter, their imposing presence accentuating the tension of the room.

Agent Collins: "Gentlemen, we are just following standard procedure. The test is a necessary step in our investigation."

Callahan: "With all due respect, Agent Collins, this test has no legal value. We request its immediate cancellation."

Agent Taylor: "The procedure is clear. If your client has nothing to hide, he shouldn't worry about taking this test."

Jim: "I have nothing to hide! But this test will prove nothing, it will only cast more doubts on my innocence."

Blake: "Jim's right. The results of these tests can be manipulated and misinterpreted. We insist that you cancel this procedure."

Collins: "We're just following orders. If you have a complaint, send it to the prosecutor."

Callahan turns to Collins, his gaze cold and determined.

Callahan: "We're going to do more than that. We are going to take legal action for obstruction of justice and harassment. My client has rights, and we will make sure that they are respected."

Taylor, slightly taken aback, exchanges a look with Collins. "This is a federal investigation. Mr. Ward is one of the prime suspects."

Collins and Taylor leave the room, leaving Jim alone with his lawyers.

Jim: "Do you really think you can cancel this test?"

Callahan: "We will do everything in our power, Jim. But you must remain calm and cooperative. Everything you say and do now can have an impact on what happens next."

Blake: "We are going to contact Richard Karter to inform him of the situation and see if he can use his influence. In the meantime, hold on tight."

The tension in the room is palpable. Jim nods, trying to stay calm despite the looming uncertainty.

Jim: "Thank you..."

The FBI agents return, accompanied by their superior.

"Gentlemen, we have heard your arguments. After discussion, we decided to suspend the lie detector test pending further examination of the situation."

Callahan: "It's a wise decision. We will appreciate an official notification of this suspension."

The FBI agents leave the room, leaving Jim, Callahan and Blake alone.

Jim: "Now what?"

Blake: "Now we need to prepare your defense in depth. Gather all the possible information and be prepared for any eventuality."

Collins: "Mr. Ward, although we have suspended the lie detector test, we must keep you for an extended interrogation. There are still many unanswered questions."

Jim: "You will see that I am telling the truth."

Collins: "We'll see, Mr. Ward. We still have a lot of questions and checks to do."

The agents leave the room, leaving Jim alone with his thoughts, still handcuffed at the table. He knows that he will have to be ready for the next steps of this intense and complicated investigation.

Alex, in his office, is bent over his laptop, scrutinizing the photos of his mother, Margaret, with Jim, which have invaded social networks. Daniel, a trusted associate, is standing by the window, his gaze directed outward.

Alex: "I leave it to Richard to make a point with my mother. In the meantime, these photos must disappear immediately. They tarnish our reputation and jeopardize our business."

Daniel: "I agree, Alex. We must contact the platforms and start a legal procedure for invasion of privacy. It might take a while, but it's our best option."

Alex: "Speaking of problems, Lucas has been arrested. Things are getting out of hand. How did we get here?"

Daniel: "It's a delicate situation. We have to face several fronts at once. What are you going to do about Lucas?"

Alex: "We have to find a way to get him out of there. But first, these photos... They must disappear. I'm going to call Callahan to come help us. He's still at the FBI office with Jim, but he should be able to reach us quickly. We need his legal expertise."

Alex calls Callahan: "Callahan, we have an urgent situation here. Photos of Margaret and Jim are circulating on social networks. Join us immediately at the Karter Finance office."

Callahan: "I'm on my way. I'll be there in ten minutes."

Alex: "We must be ready to act as soon as he arrives."

The two men go through the photos and messages online, collecting evidence to support their withdrawal request.

A little later, Callahan arrives in Alex's office.

Callahan: "Alex, Daniel, what's the latest news?"

Alex: "These photos must disappear immediately, Richard. They are harming our family."

Callahan: "We can't just make them disappear without following the proper legal procedures."

Daniel: "We have already discussed contacting the platforms and starting a legal procedure for invasion of privacy."

Callahan: "We have a strong case for invasion of privacy, especially with the notoriety of your family."

Alex: "I don't care about their procedures. Do the right thing."

Callahan: "I will contact the lawyers of the platforms and start the procedures immediately. We also have to manage crisis communication. These photos are already circulating, and we need to control the narrative before the media takes over."

Daniel: "Prepare a press release."

Alex: "I will coordinate with our public relations team to prepare the press release. We must be ready to answer all questions from the media."

Richard Karter breaks down the swinging doors of their office, visibly angry. Her features are drawn, and a gleam of betrayal shines in her eyes.

Richard: "What is this story, Alex? Pictures of Margaret with this... that Jim! What's going on here?"

Alex stands up quickly to face his father, adopting a calm and reassuring posture.

Alex: "Dad, calm down. I know it's a shock, but we are already working to resolve this situation. Maybe these photos don't mean anything. We have to make them disappear before things get out of hand."

Richard: "How can you say that, Alex? I feel betrayed. What if it was more than just an innocent encounter?"

Alex: "We don't know everything yet. Callahan is here to help us. We have already started the steps to remove the photos from social networks. Trust me, we will handle this situation."

Richard, trying to control his anger, replies: "It's already too late, Alex. We lost a major client because of this scandal. It was one of our biggest portfolios, a huge financial loss for the company."

Alex: "Which client?"

Richard: "Henderson Industries. They decided to sever all ties with us. They don't want to be associated with our name anymore, not with all these stories that are circulating."

Alex grits his teeth, realizing the extent of the damage.

Alex: "I have already put our public relations team to work to manage the crisis."

Richard: "You better. Because if we continue to lose customers at this rate, there won't be much left of Karter Finance."

Richard, still furious, leaves the office, leaving Alex, Callahan and Daniel to prepare to handle the crisis. The men disperse, each to his mission of the day, while the city takes a new restless turn.

Alex's assistant enters: "Mr. Karter, Miss Tori is here to see you."

Alex: "Let her in, please."

Tori enters the new room redeveloped by the patriarch, wearing a dress that emphasizes her slender figure, her blonde hair falling in perfect waves over her shoulders. His bright smile contrasts with Alex's preoccupied air.

Tori: "Hello, Alex. I hope I'm not bothering you, I took a little detour into town to visit you."

Alex: "Tori, come in. You never bother. What can I do for you?"

Her high heels click lightly on the floor. She sits facing Alex, crossing her legs with ease and straightening her arch.

Tori: "I know things are difficult right now, especially with Lucas in prison. They are talking about it in all the media in the city, it feels like the events are out of control. I wanted to offer you my help."

Alex: "Your help?"

Tori: "Yes, as a lawyer. I can defend Lucas. I know his case well and I am sure I can bring a different perspective."

Alex observes Tori, noting the determination in her eyes. She has always been bright and ambitious, and he knows that she could really make a difference.

Alex: "That's very generous of you, Tori. But you know it's not an easy matter. Lucas is accused of concealing evidence, and the evidence against him is strong."

Tori: "I know it well, Alex. But I believe

in his innocence, and I am ready to fight for him. Moreover, I think that he is a victim of political manipulation. We have to give him a fair chance."

Tori gets up and moves closer to Alex, putting her hand on his shoulder and sticking against him.

Alex: "Okay, Tori. If you're willing to take that risk, I trust you. Lucas needs all the help he can get."

Tori smiles, a mixture of satisfaction and determination on her face.

Tori: "Thank you, Alex. I won't disappoint you."

Alex: "I don't doubt it. Just make sure you have all the details. This case is more complex than it seems."

Tori: "I'm going to dive into it immediately. And don't worry, I'm ready to face whatever stands in our way."

Alex sighs and takes a deep breath.

Alex: "Tori, that's not all. We lost a major client because of this scandal. Henderson Industries has severed all ties with us. It was one of our biggest portfolios. The economic situation of Karter Finance is about to falter."

Tori widens her eyes, taking in the seriousness of the situation. She thinks for a moment, then makes a bold decision.

Tori: "Alex, since I have touched my mother's inheritance, I have considerable financial resources. If you allow it, I could invest in Karter Finance. I want to be more than just a lawyer for this family. I want to be a shareholder and help stabilize the company."

Alex looks at Tori, surprised by her proposal. He sees the determination in her eyes and understands that she is sincere.

Alex: "That's an interesting proposal, Tori. It will have to be discussed with my father, but I think it could be beneficial for everyone. Thank you for your support."

Tori: "I am ready to fully commit. Let me know when you want to talk to Richard about it."

Alex: "I will. We will talk about it soon. Thanks again, Tori. Your proposal shows how much you care about us."

The local media, eager for scandals, never stopped relaying rumors and allegations. Tori's arrival brought a breath of fresh air. His proposal to defend Lucas testified to his unwavering dedication and his willingness to thwart the political maneuvers and manipulations at stake.

But it was his suggestion to invest in Karter Finance, using his mother's inheritance, that resonated deeply with Alex. This bold, unexpected offer was a clear sign of his commitment to their side in this fierce battle. Alex, although surprised, welcomed this proposal with a recognition mixed with relief. He knew that his father Richard's approval would be crucial, but he could already see a glimmer of hope breaking through the dark clouds.

Alex's state of mind at that moment was a complex mixture of hope and determination. The betrayals, the manipulations, and the financial stakes weighed heavily on his shoulders, but he knew that with Tori by their side, they had a chance to sail through this storm. The prospect of Tori's investment, combined with her unwavering support, offered a new strategy to counter the forces that sought to take them down.

As Tori left the office, Alex felt ready to face the challenges ahead. The road would be long and fraught with difficulties, but he was determined to protect his family and their business, at all costs.

Tori's determination and unwavering commitment gave Alex the strength to fight against the intrigues and betrayals that threatened their world.

CHAPTER 7

THE FAMILY AFFAIR

The next day Tori goes to the prison with an unshakable determination and a well-prepared legal strategy.

The prison has an oppressive atmosphere. Tori, dressed in an elegant black suit that emphasizes her slender figure, walks through the heavy metal doors. His imposing appearance and his assured gait attract attending guards and inmates. A guard directed Tori to the visiting room, where Lucas had already taken his position behind thick glass. When he looks up and sees her enter, his face shows surprise.

Tori sits across from Lucas, putting her documents on the table. She takes a moment to observe Lucas, noting the signs of fatigue on his face.

Tori: "Hello Lucas, I spoke to the judge and I have good news. We get you out on bail. But you have to keep cooperating.'

Lucas, exhausted since his arrest,

Lucas: "Thank you, Tori. And thank you to Alex for agreeing to take over my deposit. "

Tori gives a slight smile, trying to reassure Lucas.

Tori: "Alex is a very generous person for his friends. We prove you are the victim of political manipulation. They want to silence you because you are too close to the truth."

She opens her file, revealing a multitude of legal documents and detailed notes.

Tori: "I've already started preparing your defense. Tell me everything about your sources and your knowledge. The more information I have, the more solid a case we can build."

Lucas looks down, struggling with his conscience.

Lucas: "Tori, there are some things I can't say... to protect my sources."

Tori, her gaze becoming more intense,

Tori: "But if you don't tell me everything, we won't have enough ammunition to defend you. Trust me, I'm here to help you."

She puts a reassuring hand on the glass that separates them, seeking to establish a bond of trust and solidarity.

Tori: "We're going to make it, Lucas. We can still do a lot to prove your innocence and expose political manipulations.

Lucas takes a deep breath, then nods.

Lucas: "Okay. I'll tell you everything. But promise me to protect my sources."

Tori: "I promise."

She pulls out a pen and a notebook, ready to record everything.

Tori: "Let's start from the beginning. Share with me your findings and the process behind your conclusions.

Lucas speaks, his voice trembling at first, then gaining in confidence as he confides. Tori listens, taking detailed notes and asking specific questions to clarify each point.

Lucas: "I discovered that several financial transactions went through shell companies. They transferred the funds to offshore accounts, and some influential politicians were associated with these accounts."

Tori: "Do you have any concrete evidence of these transactions? Documents, recordings?"

Lucas: "Yes, I have copies of bank statements and audio recordings of incriminating conversations and the FBI has them too."

Tori nods, satisfied with the solidity of the evidence.

Tori: "All right. We are going to use this information to show that you have only done your job as a journalist by revealing facts and that you have also contributed to helping the federal authorities. We also have to prove that your arrest is an attempt to silence you."

She closes her notebook, her gaze fixed on Lucas.

Tori: "I'm going to present this evidence to the judge and argue in your favor to get you released on bail."

Lucas, despite the fatigue, feels a glimmer of hope reborn in him.

Tori stands up, adjusting her suit to her wasp waist, ready to go.

She shakes Lucas's hand through the glass, a silent promise not to give up. While she leaves the prison.

In the Karter's home, the family has been feeling a gloomy atmosphere since Jim's arrest because of the photos that were made public a few hours ago on social networks. Richard Karter, in an cut suit, paces the living room, express anger and betrayal engraved on his face. The house, quiet and, seems today reflecting Richard's inner storm.

Margaret, sitting on the sofa with a glass of alcohol in her hand resting on the armrest, tries to maintain her calm despite the rumbling storm. She knows that confrontation is inevitable. Richard turns to her, his eyes shooting flashes.

Richard: "Margaret, you believed I would never find out about this... this betrayal? Pictures of you and Jim, outside his house, in this compromising situation! Your defense? What is it?"

Margaret, taking a sip, stands up slowly. She knows that every word counts and that the slightest mistake could make the situation worse.

Margaret: "Richard, it's not what you think. Jim is an old friend, and this appointment was nothing personal. We were talking business, nothing more."

Richard: "Business? In light clothes and messy hair, at his place? Are you kidding me? Do you think I'm blind or just stupid?"

Margaret tries to remain calm, but the pain of betrayal and humiliation rises in her.

Margaret: "I know it sounds compromising, but I assure you, there was nothing more than banal discussions. Jim's in a tough spot and needs advice.

Richard: "Any advice? And you became his mentor, right? Don't take your excuses for truths, Margaret. How could you do this to me? To me, to our family?"

Margaret's face is wet with tears, but she refuses to allow the emotion to overwhelm her.

Margaret: "Richard, I'm sorry if this hurt you. That was never my intention. You must understand, you are not always present either. You're engrossed in work, and sometimes I feel lonely..."

Richard, furious, brushes off his statement with a gesture.

Richard: "Don't turn the situation around, Margaret. It's not an excuse for what you did. You broke my trust, and even worse, you tarnished our public image. The media are already reveling in this scandal, and we are losing customers because of you!"

Margaret: "I never wanted to betray you, Richard. You are the man I love, but we must face this crisis together. We have to set a higher standard."

Richard: "Together? How can you pronounce this word after what you've done?"

Margaret, seeking reconciliation.

Margaret: "Richard, I know it's hard to believe, but I'm willing to do anything to fix this. For us, for our family. Give me a chance to prove that I am worthy of your trust."

Richard: "Prove your trust? Come again? By remaining faithful this time?"

Richard's words are like knives, cutting deep into Margaret's soul.

Margaret: "I will do whatever it takes. I will submit to all the conditions that you impose. But don't reject me. Don't let us sink because of this mistake."

Richard, his features distorted by anger and pain, turns his back on Margaret, staring into the void.

Margaret: "Why don't you ask Jim? He will tell you the truth."

Margaret's words trigger a fresh wave of anger in Richard.

Richard: "Jim? How could I still trust this man? He was my closest friend, and now I doubt everything about him, including in business. He betrayed me as much as you did."

The silence falls, heavy and oppressive. Margaret, in despair, tries one last time to reason with him.

Richard: "I don't know if I can forgive you, Margaret. Not now. But for now, we need to salvage whatever we can from our company and our reputation. We'll talk about ourselves later. I advise you to make your time useful to our parish in Greenwood Hills, but don't seduce our priest!'

Margaret: "Thank you, Richard. Thank you for not giving up."

In the meeting room of the FBI office, Collins and Taylor stood side by side, their faces illuminated by the glow of computer screens that projected a mixture of financial documents, photographs and call records. Notes and arrows covered the surrounding whiteboards, connecting various names, dates, and places, forming a labyrinth of complex connections.

The agents, deeply engrossed in their reflections, focused on analyzing the additional evidence. The financial analyst, who had spent hours digging through the intricacies of banking transactions, waved to Collins to get his attention.

"We have discovered some unusual financial movements," he began, his index finger pointing at the screen. "Significant amounts of money transferred between Jim Ward's accounts and several shell companies based in Florida. These companies seem to be fronts for money laundering operations."

Collins nodded, poring over the details of the transfers. The amounts were significant, and the transactions, scattered over several months, suggested a well-established network.

"This confirms our suspicions," Collins declared, his tone full of gravity. "Jim is involved in something much larger than he lets on. It's time to inspect his relationships and motives."

Taylor, who was taking notes next door, added: "And there is this name that comes up often: Victor Dubois. This alias is infamous in the criminal realm. His activities cover international financial traffic, and he uses his connections to maintain a legitimate facade."

The analyst nodded. "Dubois uses his skills to navigate between the cracks. He is involved in transactions that go beyond our borders, with links as far as Europe and Asia."

Collins thinks for a moment, weighing the weight of this new information. Margaret's knowledge of Jim's operations could unravel this affair.

Taylor intervened, saying, "We have to explore this lead." Margaret might have crucial information about Jim, even if she's not involved.

The analyst added: "And there is also Harris. The analyst mentioned that our research shows a potential link between Harris and acts of real estate corruption. He added Harris used his influences to hide illegal operations. It is possible that Jim acted as an intermediary in some of these transactions."

Unease filled the room as the investigation's magnitude grew clear. Each new discovery brought its share of complexity, weaving a network of intrigues where each actor played a crucial role.

"Good," Collins concludes, getting up. "We have a lot to do." We have to ask Jim again, dig into Margaret and her relationships with him, and above all, not lose sight of Dubois and Harris. They live in this labyrinth.

Taylor nodded. "Jim remains in custody at the moment. We need to use this time to strengthen our case, explore every corner of its connections, and put pressure on where it will crack this network."

The FBI agents knew the path would be arduous, but each discovery brought them closer to the truth. In this game of chess, every move mattered, and they were determined to expose the secrets buried under the deceptive appearances of the elites of Greenwood Hills. The web of corruption, betrayal, and shenanigans was closing in. Time to find out who would fall first.

In the hushed atmosphere of the courtroom, the tension was palpable. Tori, dressed in a suit that emphasized her stature as a lawyer, advanced with a determined gait towards the center of the room. All around, the murmur of journalists, lawyers and curious people testified to the intense interest that Lucas Bennett's case aroused. This trial, beyond its personal stake for the journalist, embodied a larger struggle between truth and political manipulation.

Lucas, sitting next to his lawyer, was watching the scene. The sudden arrest had shaken his world. Everyone knew about Tori's tenacity and strategic flair, and today she was ready to prove that Lucas was the victim of a conspiracy with wider ramifications than those presented.

The imposing courtroom reinforced the moment itself, with its high, ornate ceilings and dark wooden walls. Tense faces filled the benches, anticipating the events that were about to unfold.

The judge sat behind the large wooden desk, attentive and analytical.

Tori stood in front of him, her notes organized, each argument prepared with the precision of a surgeon. Last night, she diligently studied documents, searching for precedents, constructing a defense to prove Lucas's innocence and expose his manipulators.

In presenting her case, Tori showed a captivating eloquence. Tori exposed the flaws in the accusations against Lucas, revealing how political opponents had fabricated the charges to silence one of the few journalists still capable of uncovering the truth. She chose each word and constructed each sentence to maximize the impact of her demonstration. The tone of his voice, both firm and passionate, captured attending the audience, uniting the spectators in a concentrated listening.

She highlighted Lucas' deep roots in the community, emphasizing his integrity and commitment to the truth. Despite appearances, he was a principled man caught in a power-abuse conspiracy.

His lips held the room captive. Skepticism once filled the faces of the spectators, but soon transformed into expressions of deep reflection. With increasing interest, the attentive jurors noted every detail. Tori's performance was masterful, not only because she tackled the inconsistencies of the file, but because she breathed a soul into her argument, a lively force that few could ignore.

The judge listened with sustained attention, his stern features betraying the growing interest he took in Tori's argument. He recognized in her a formidable opponent, someone who would not settle for half measures to defend her client.

As Tori progressed in her demonstration, she evoked the tangible evidence of the abuses of power orchestrated by those who wanted to silence Lucas. As Tori progressed in her demonstration, she exposed the bias in each accusation and revealed how those who wanted to silence Lucas had compromised the integrity of investigating the start.

"Your Honor," she began, her clear voice cutting the air like a blade, "I request permission to call Inspector Mitchell to the stand to clarify certain aspects of this case that, so far, have remained in the shadows."

The judge, a man of imposing stature, nodded. "Permission granted, Master Tori."

A murmur ran through the room as Inspector Mitchell rose from his seat. She approached the witness chair with a firm gait, but her eyes revealed tension.

"Detective Mitchell," Tori said with a calm but inflexible voice, "Can you explain to us the circumstances of the arrest of Lucas Bennett? And more precisely, what external influences may have influenced your decision?"

Mitchell, upright in her seat, hesitated for a moment. "The evidence was solid," she replied, trying to keep an imperturbable facade.

"Solid, you say?" Tori retorted, her piercing gaze fixed on Mitchell. "However, it would seem that political pressures have played a significant role. Pressures coming from influential people like Harris, aren't they?"

The mention of Harris caused a shudder in the assembly. Tori intensified her point.

"Inspector Mitchell, have you received instructions from people at the top of the political pyramid to take action against my client?"

Mitchell bowed his head, the weight of Tori's questions seeming to weigh on his shoulders. "Some... discussions have taken place," she admitted, her words measured.

"Discussions, yes," Tori continued. "But weren't they rather ordered? Instructions to harm a journalist seeking truth?"

Mitchell opened his mouth to retort, but Tori didn't give him the opportunity. She turned to the judge, the intensity of her speech having not diminished one iota.

"Your Honor, it is crucial that this court understands the extent of the political manipulations that led to the arrest of Lucas Bennett. The evidence we have presented shows not only his innocence but also the vast plot orchestrated to silence him."

The judge observed Mitchell, then turned back to Tori. "Proceed, Master Tori," he uttered, the weight of his words lingering in the room.

"Lucas Bennett is a respected journalist, rooted in this community," Tori insisted. His sole mistake was revealing truths that certain individuals wished to conceal. His arrest is nothing more than an act of political revenge."

Silence fell again in the courtroom, each spectator holding his breath. Tori revealed a truth that few had confronted.

"Your Honor," she concluded, "I urge this court to consider these external influences and recognize that Lucas Bennett is innocent of the charges against him."

The judge leaned forward, his fingers crossed on the desk. "I will take the time to examine the elements presented here today. The judge leaned forward, crossing his fingers on the desk.

As Tori returned to her place, feel discreet triumph accompanied her. She had introduced doubt where certainty reigned, and she knew that every word spoken today could influence Lucas's future.

Lucas, sitting at the defense table, observed Tori with visible recognition. He recognized her as a determined lawyer and a valuable ally in the search for the truth. Tori planted doubt in the judge's mind. Now we wait for justice.

Spectators, aware of the significance, made the room silent. The suspense was at its height, a palpable tension that seemed almost electric. Murmurs silenced, all awaited the judge's verdict with feverish expectation.

When Tori concluded, she cast a confident glance at Lucas. She had fought a hard fight, convinced that she had sown doubt in the minds of the judge and the jurors. She returned to her place, her heart pounding but her face serene, knowing that she had given everything she had to save Lucas.

The judge pondered his words, his decision heavy in the air. The wait was unbearable, every second stretching into eternity. Before the verdict, a glimmer of hope appeared. Tori had planted a seed of truth, a challenge to the darkness that threatened to engulf Lucas and his fight for justice.

The restaurant was overflowing with refined elegance, each table carefully set up to host discussions where power and money mingled.

Richard Karter and his son Alex entered the room, an imposing duo with their confident appearance and their undeniable presence. Richard wore a fitted suit, his graying hair coiffed, while Alex, at his side, sported a natural elegance that came from his father. Their entrance attracted a few glances, recognizing the business magnate and his prodigal son.

They went to a table in a hidden corner, where a confident woman awaited them. She was wearing a sober but elegant black dress.

Richard: "Hello. I hope you haven't waited too long."

Emma: "Not at all, Mr. Karter. I am delighted that you have accepted this meeting."

Richard took his seat, his gaze assessing Emma's every gesture, trying to understand the intentions behind this invitation. The server brought a bottle of wine, which Emma had chosen, and filled the glasses. Alex, intrigued and on guard, wondered about the meaning of this meeting.

Emma: "I'm here to discuss an opportunity. I represent a competing group interested in Karter Finance."

Richard: "An opportunity? The shares of my company are not for sale. You should know that."

Emma: "Everyone has a price, Richard. Just find it."

Richard gave Alex a furtive look, looking for some form of tacit support. Her son, although silent.

Emma considers more than just buying. Maybe even something personal. Gentlemen, isn't it beautiful to combine staff and family?"

Richard: "No one goes into a deal without knowing the other party. What are you hiding?"

Emma paused, letting the tension settle in. She had prepared for this moment, turning it into a orchestrated revelation.

Emma: "I know details about your company that few people know, Richard. Including personal details that could harm you if revealed."

Alex: "What details are you talking about?"

Emma suggests keeping certain details confidential, especially given the current circumstances involving you. Imagine the scandal that someone could cause if they revealed these details, especially in the current times concerning you. I imagine you are still avoiding a recent scandal."

Richard felt his heart quicken. This woman was playing a dangerous game, and he didn't enjoy being the one whose rules escaped him. He despised the idea of relying on a stranger, especially in public.

Richard: "If you think you can blackmail me, think again."

Emma: "I'm not here for blackmail, Richard. I demand what belongs to me. I'm Emma, your daughter."

A shocking silence settled, like a silent shock wave that passed through the table. Richard felt vulnerable, as if the ground had slipped under his feet. Emma's every word carried a truth that he could not ignore, and he faced a past that he had buried. Alex, wide-eyed, turned to his father, the gravity of the situation becoming clear.

Alex: "So, I would have a stepsister, dad!? Explain yourself."

The revelation left Richard stunned, his mind searching for scraps of memories that could confirm or disprove Emma's words. It was a blow he hadn't seen coming, a ghost from the past popping up to claim his due.

Emma, sitting opposite them, kept her calm while waiting for what she could win at the exchange.

Emma: "I don't want to be your enemy. I want to be a partner. I can be an asset, or a formidable opponent."

Richard said, "Emma." I won't allow the daughter of my ex-wife, who has already tried to use my credit card without permission, to dictate to me. What a hypocrite she is, sending her daughter to attack me.

Emma: 'I'm your daughter too. You'll have to get used to it now,'

During the conversation, Richard realized his life would change forever. He now had to deal with a hidden daughter and dangerous alliances. Alex, by his side, understood that this family battle would change Karter's future and was more uncertain than ever.

Richard recalled vague memories of forgotten liaisons. He realized that the mistakes of his past had very real repercussions and that he could no longer ignore them. Emma's gaze served as a constant reminder of his neglect and lost opportunities.

The afternoon sun bathed the city in its golden light as Richard and Alex left the restaurant, leaving behind the tumult of revelations. In the air-conditioned passenger compartment of the car, Richard's driver kept his eyes on the road, navigating through the busy traffic with silent precision.

Alex was sitting in the back, lost in his thoughts, his gaze fixed on the streets that were passing in front of him. The recent meeting with Emma had ignited in him a flame of ambition, a burning desire to reassert himself as a leader within Karter Finance.

The mention of potential new partners in Panama aroused in him a renewed determination. He saw this as an opportunity to redefine his role in front of his half-sister, to prove that he was ready to take over the family torch with vigor and vision.

In the passenger seat, Richard seemed pensive, his rigid posture betraying the inner hurricane that tormented him. His meeting with Emma, this girl whose existence he did not know, had been a shock that shook the very foundations of his existence. Accepting the resurfaced past was tough, but facing consequences was necessary.

The muffled sounds of traffic seemed distant, almost unreal, as Richard turned to his son. Alex, although immersed in his reflections, felt the weight of his father's gaze. A silent but meaningful exchange was taking place between them, a tacit understanding of the challenges ahead.

Integrating this new reality into his life, Alex contemplated the existence of a half-sister. This revelation had shaken him, but it had also stoked his determination to take the reins of his professional future with renewed confidence. By taking on the projects in Panama, he hoped to prove to his father, his family, and himself that he was prepared to make the hard choices required to lead Karter Finance to greater success and distance himself from his scandals and negative influences.

Announcing Lucas' release was today's good news.

During the ride along the tree-lined avenues, Alex let his mind wander towards the strategies that could enhance the company's global standing. Not only was the prospect of working with the partners in Panama a stimulating challenge, but it also promised growth and innovation.

Richard, for his part, was thinking about how to manage this new family dynamic. Emma's presence in his life posed hard questions, and he knew he had to navigate these troubled waters while protecting his business and his family. Facing the reality of his daughter becoming a business opponent required pragmatism and composure.

Alex said, "You know, Dad, Tori's proposal went well." Her offer seems healthier to me than Emma's. This won't give Emma an advantage.

Richard said, "Of course, my son. Call her and let her come."

The vehicle halted at their residence. As the driver opened the door, Richard and Alex exchanged a knowing glance, aware that new secrets would shape their bond.

The gate opened, letting Tori's car pass, which was driving to the entrance. As she got out of her vehicle, she took a moment to admire the imposing architecture of the manor, a perfect fusion between tradition and modernity. Her heart beat faster at the thought of what was waiting for her inside.

Her dream was to play a significant role in the business world, not just as a lawyer. His ambition and determination validated when he stood at the door of the Karters. She was on the verge of becoming a crucial player in the fate of a highly influential family in Greenwood Hills, which brought her newfound energy.

As she walked through the vestibule, she noticed the opulent details that defined each room: dangling crystal chandeliers, patterned Persian carpets, and original works of art hanging on the walls. The house exuded a timeless elegance, testifying to the heritage and the refined taste of the Karter family.

Inflated with feel abundant wealth, she headed for the living room where the meeting was being held, each step bringing her a little closer to achieving her ambitions. As she crossed the threshold, she met Alex, who greeted her with a grateful smile.

"As they left the room, Alex thanked Tori for her skillful defense of Lucas. 'Thanks to you, we could keep Lucas with us. "

Despite the recent pressures and scandals, he exuded an aura of unshakable confidence, ready to listen to what Tori offered.

Alex and Tori took their seats next to each other, and Tori stated her proposal. She knew that convincing Richard Karter would not be a simple task, but she was determined to play an active role in the revival of Karter Finance and especially after conquering Alex, it was her father's turn.

"Richard, I understand the challenges that Karter Finance is facing," she began, her tone full of sincerity. That's why I want to invest. With the funds from my mother's inheritance, I can provide significant financial support that would help stabilize our operations and strengthen our position in the market. »

Richard stared at Tori, weighing every word. Although he suspected the new alliances since the trap that Emma had set for him.

"And what would you ask, Tori? "He asked with a raised eyebrow.

Tori answered without hesitation, aware of prizing this moment. "I want to become a shareholder. I believe in the value of Karter Finance and am ready to engage in the company's strategy. I think that my perspective could be a valuable asset, especially for our ambitions on the Panama market Alex told me about. »

Alex intervened, feeling the need to support Tori. He knew she brought not only funds but also her presence, which brings him a sentimental affection.

"Dad, Tori has proven time and time again that she is a trusted ally," he added, his gaze shifting from his father to Tori. "His investment could not only help us get through this crisis but also rebuild our reputation." His contribution would give all the strength and credibility necessary for the Panama market, where we have promising projects. »

Tori smiles, determined. "I welcome this opportunity." Panama represents a new frontier for Karter Finance, and I am convinced that we can achieve great things together there. »

Richard remained silent, absorbed in reflection. He understood the decision's significance for Karter Finance's future. Being the family head and company leader, he had to consider risks and opportunities.

After a moment of contemplation, he stood up, looking out the window, seeing his wife tending her roses.

"Very well, Tori," he finally declared, his voice full of solemn gravity. "If you are ready to make a full commitment and respect the values of Karter Finance, I am ready to accept your offer and in addition, you will always be useful as a lawyer.'

Tori nodded, her face beaming with gratitude and a well-organized accomplishment.

The meeting ended on a note of cautious optimism. Richard, Alex, and Tori give each other warm cordial hugs, and Richard proposes in a victorious tone.

"Alex, Tori how about you celebrate all this!, also invite your journalist. I will order him a better article than his gossip that he published that will wash his notoriety. "

As the festive evening starts, the final reddish rays mark a new era for the Karter family. The streets were lively, the most beautiful cars were showing off and strutting around. A chic restaurant, perfect for celebrating victories, was at the center of this effervescence.

Alex, Richard, Tori, and Lucas gathered around the table, capturing attending the surrounding guests with their presence. Their laughter and lively conversations formed a symphony of joy and relief.

"Get the champagne flowing! " He cries out, the bill is for Richard.

Tori, dressed in an elegant dress that hugged her figure, savored every moment of this celebration. Her eyes sparkle with excitement, not only because she had integrated the Karter family's business but also because she felt a genuine camaraderie with her new partners. She stood close to Alex, her hand brushing his arm, sharing a knowing look that testified to a budding intimacy and a deep connection. Every smile exchanged, every toast made to their success reinforced his sense of belonging.

Richard celebrates the success of Tori and the release of Lucas, but also for the new phase of Karter Finance. Looking around, he saw realizing his efforts and the promise of a prosperous future for the family business. With a satisfied smile, he raised his glass for a toast, omitting even in his thoughts of Jim and Margaret.

"To our shared success and the bright future that awaits us." Thank you all for being here tonight to celebrate these moments of triumph and renewal. "

Alex, sitting next to Tori, allowed her friend to set her on fire and then raised her glass, adding with a touch of pride,

"To Lucas newfound freedom, to Tori's triumphant entry into our affairs, and to our father, Richard, for his wisdom and tenacity."

A heartwarming smile spread across Lucas face as he felt an overwhelming sense of gratitude for the support he received during challenging moments. The release had marked a new stage for him, a second chance to prove his worth. Raising his glass, he declared,

We all believe in the truth's triumph.

Their glasses clashed in a joyful tinkle, sealing an evening of shared promises and dreams.

Richard took advantage of this moment to approach Lucas.

"Lucas, I have a new mission for you. I would like you to write an article about the challenges and opportunities of the Karter finance financial market. Seize the chance to showcase Karter Finance and yourself. »

Lucas, delighted to receive this new mission, nodded.

Throughout the evening, the closeness between Tori and Alex became more and more clear. She put her hand on his, laughing at his jokes, leaned towards him to whisper audible words, creating a bubble around them in which the rest of the world seemed to faint. Alex appreciated this attention, feeling that the alliance between them would not only be professional but also personal.

That night, in the vibrant heart of the city, the Karter family and their allies sealed a pact of friendship and ambition.

The dark cases of murders and ongoing investigations seemed to fade away, replaced by the flamboyant ambitions and the financial prospects that awaited them. Yet beneath the surface, the hidden truths remained ready to resurface at any moment.

CHAPTER 8

A NEW DAWN KARTER

I n the FBI interrogation room, the atmosphere was heavy with tension and unsaid. The gray walls and the low lighting only stressed the seriousness of the situation. Jim Ward, handcuffed, was sitting at a metal table, his eyes scanning those of Agents Collins and Taylor, who stood in front of him.

Jim felt the pressure mounting, but he knew that his cooperation was his only hope of reducing his sentence. He had played his cards, aware that every word could have important consequences.

"Listen," he began, his voice betraying a mixture of defiance and resignation. "I am ready to give you the information you need, but I want a guarantee of reducing my sentence."

Agent Collins, impassive, observed Jim with an appraising look. He knew he was dealing with a man in distress, but he needed hard evidence to move forward.

"Jim, we might consider an arrangement, but only if what you offer is valuable enough to dismantle the network," Collins replied.

Jim launches into his revelations.

"Harris orchestrated evaluating the land to gain it at a cheap price," explained Jim. "He has plans for a private airfield and a luxury retirement home. All this by manipulating prices with illegal methods and using shell companies to hide his intentions."

Agent Taylor was taking notes while listening. "The transactions between your accounts and these companies in Florida are suspicious, Jim. Can you explain these financial movements?"

Jim paused, choosing his words. "It was a facade. Harris wanted Karter Finance to manage his funds to give appear legitimacy. Margaret advised me to use Karter Finance for this, but she didn't know about the fraud."

Taylor exchanged a glance with Collins, noting the repeated mention of Margaret. "We have heard that. Let's talk about Marcus Hale. What role did he play?"

Jim passed a hand over his face, his tired features testifying to his inner struggle. "Marcus was laundering the money for Harris. The money flowed from Florida to Greenwood Hills, then returned to Harris as commissions. Marcus was the intermediary, the indispensable cog in this system."

Officer Collins put down his pen, reflecting on the situation. "And you, Jim? What motivated your involvement in this case?"

Jim. "Harris promised me a stake in one of his companies. It was supposed to secure my future, but now I see it was a mistake."

Collins, in an incisive tone, continued: "Let's talk about the murders of Mrs. Blackwood and Farwell. Who sponsored these acts?"

Jim stated that he didn't know who gave the order, but he knew these people were disrupting the status quo. There is a henchman, someone who performs dirty tasks on behalf of the powerful."

Taylor, interested, stepped forward: "Do you think Harris has an enforcer? Someone who removes obstacles?"

Jim looked at Taylor: "Harris is someone who avoids doing any hands-on work. He lets the others do the dirty work and stays in the shadows."

Collins thinks for a moment, absorbing this revelation. Then, he made an important decision: "Jim, if you will cooperate fully, we could offer you witness protection."

Jim looked up, surprised. The idea of witness protection was an unexpected lifeline. In the US, witness protection is highly secure, providing a new identity and relocation for those who testify against criminals.

Collins continued, explaining the details: "This means that we will place you in a secure program. We'll give you a new identity and shield you from retribution."

Jim took a moment to consider this option. Despite knowing the risks, he found the allure of a new, threat-free life with the authorities appealing.

"I am ready to cooperate," he finally said.

Taylor acknowledging the legitimacy of Jim's request: "We will do everything in our power to ensure the safety of you and your loved ones. But we need your help to ensure that justice is served."

Jim felt a weight ease from his shoulders. Despite knowing he wasn't free from the deal, he considered cooperating as a potential escape from this nightmare.

The interrogation continued, each question bringing its share of revelations about the complexity of Harris' criminal network. Jim realized that his only chance of redemption was to provide valuable help to the investigators.

Time is running out, the investigation is almost over. Every minute was unbearable to live. Moments like these condemn evil forever. The Karter family is like the others, human nature with its primary sides, the facets of the vices of this humanity that try to be reborn in forgiveness.

Forgiving yourself would be easier than forgiving the other.

For these two lovers, the page will turn to other horizons by leaving their memory of ecstasies hidden by their silk sheet that discovered the bodies of desire in lies.

Margaret Karter entered the detention center, the metallic sounds of the doors closing behind her marking every step of her way to Jim. The choice to come here burdened her, but she accepted the inevitable confrontation.

Jim Ward, however, waited. His face, marked by drawn features, reflected the shadow of his former confidence. His eyes, usually bright, were dull, marked by anguish and regret.

Margaret remembered their promises, the moments of complicity from a different time. Betrayal created an unbridgeable gap, a timeless abyss between them. She spoke, her voice betraying at the same time the pain.

"Jim, everything we had is over now. Your betrayal destroyed everything."

Jim nodded, his shoulders sagging under the weight of his guilt. "I know, Margaret. And I regret everything I did."

She felt sadness come over her, but she knew she had to stay strong. "We could have built something real, but you chose deception and manipulation. Now you have to live with the consequences of your actions."

Jim searching for the words to express what he was feeling. "I am in witness protection now. I agreed to talk for security. Maybe one day you'll be able to forgive me."

Silence enveloped them, carrying the weight of everything left unsaid. Margaret understood that this confession was Jim's last attempt to find some kind of redemption. Unsure if she could ever forgive him, she knew she had to move on.

Embracing a life without lies or pretense, she stood up. Her last look, hoping to see her past love, met only a stranger.

"Goodbye, Jim," she said, her voice calm but firm. "I wish you to find peace, but I must now seek my own."

The farewell had been painful, but necessary she was determined to rebuild herself, protect her family and move on.

Jim watched as Margaret departed, aware it was their final encounter. The words "farewell" echoed in his head, marking the end of an opulent era. He knew cooperating with authorities was his sole chance for redemption and to start anew.

Karter Finance headquarters hosts critical meeting shaping the company's future.

Board members assembled around a table in the conference room. Alex Karter, heir and visionary, presided over meeting confidence, his piercing gaze sweeping the assembly with a natural authority.

Richard Karter, the founder of the family dynasty and a true pillar of the company, sat to Alex's right, while Tori Blackwood, integrated into the members, represented the renewal and the energy that Karter Finance needed.

Alex stood up his voice resonates with a clarity that captivated everyone's attention.

"Dear Board members," he began, "we are at the dawn of a new era for Karter Finance. After trials that have tested our resilience, today we are ready to seize the opportunities that present themselves to us. Including Tori Blackwood on our board of directors marks a decisive turning point.

The project in Panama is not simply extend our current operations, but a real transformation for Karter Finance. Our goal is straightforward: to raise $100 million in order to secure strategic land and launch essential infrastructure construction.

All the members applaud Alex and exchange smiles, along with self-congratulations.

Alex paused, letting his words imprint themselves in everyone's mind.

"Panama, with its expanding economy and attractive tax incentives, is fertile ground for our ambitions. The Panamanian real estate market is booming, with a projected increase of 15% over the next five years. This favorable context offers us the opportunity to invest and achieve significant returns."

He supported his speech with relevant comparisons to illustrate the potential impact of the project.

"Let's take, for example, Pearson Capital, which led a similar fundraising in Dubai, generating an impressive 20% return in just two years. This success illustrates what we can achieve in Panama."

Alex turned to the screen behind him, displaying financial projections and strategic partnerships that reinforced his vision.

"By investing in this project, our partners can expect a return on investment of 18% per year, supported by solid guarantees and rigorous risk management. We have already established alliances with industry leaders to ensure the long-term success of this initiative."

To conclude his intervention on a positive note, Alex announced,

"We are at the dawn of a new era for Karter Finance. With the support of the Council, we are ready to take this decisive step and to inscribe our name among the pioneers of international expansion. And the trip to meet our investors in Panama is in preparation. These meetings will be crucial to complete our ambitions and guarantee the success of our project."

Alex and his determination to move forward with confidence, assuring the company and its partners that each stage of the project maximizes the opportunities for success.

The eyes turned to Tori, who greeted attending a bright smile. She then spoke, expressing her gratitude and her vision for the future of the company.

"I am honored to join your family," she said with conviction. "The expansion project in Panama represents not only an opportunity for growth but also a chance to redefine our presence on the international scene. My personal investment is a testament to my faith in our collective potential."

Richard, observing the scene with satisfaction, added, "Tori brings a fresh perspective and innovative ideas that will strengthen our position, and she contributes more than just her capital alone."

The meeting climaxed when the members submitted the vote for Tori's official inclusion on the board of directors.the members voted in favor of his appointment, thus sealing a promising Alliance for the Future of Karter Finance.

Alex expressed satisfaction. "Your trust in Tori and our strategic plan is a sign that we are on the right track. With her among us, we have given a new impetus to our vision. She will play a crucial role in our efforts to conquer new markets and solidify our reputation."

Tori, moved but determined, accepted the responsibility with humility and ambition. His appointment symbolized a renewal for the company and a commitment to the future.

Richard, eager to capitalize on this moment of optimism, spoke to conclude: "an article will soon appear in the press, highlighting our efforts and our recent successes. This will help to restore our image and strengthen the trust of our partners and customers."

The meeting ended on a note of renewed confidence and hope to the Karter with renewed applause.

Alex, Richard, Tori, and Lucas sat around the table. He, Alex, was having lunch and working on the hard-hitting article for the Greenwood Hills Journal, which had become the agenda.

The conversation ignited as they embarked on a delirious brainstorming to find the perfect title for the article. The room was echoing with laughter and mischievous comments.

Alex, with a playful grin, spoke up: "Alright, folks, we need to think creatively." How do you feel about 'Karter Finance: The Architects of the New World?"

Tori, enthusiastic, added: "Or even better, 'Karter Finance: The Magicians of the Millions'. It's catchy and mysterious, don't you think? »

Lucas, who loved pushing ideas to the extreme, exclaimed: "And why not 'Karter Finance: The Alchemists of Fortune'?" We will turn your dreams into pure gold! "

Richard, amused, retorted: "It almost sounds like a reality TV program, but I love it!" Maybe I should buy myself a magician's cape for the occasion. "

Tori dramatically pointed at Richard and said: "Imagine Mr. Richard Karter, a master of finance and politics, a visionary who merges art and economics."

Richard, laughing, said: "Isn't it a little pompous?" Sounds like a politician's speech! But I could always play the role of the wise mentor who guides young talents."

Alex added: "Let's not get carried away with greatness, otherwise we'll end up calling it 'Karter Finance: The Saviors of the Financial World.'"

Delighted with the turn of events, Tori proposed: "How about we take it even further?" Karter Finance: Because we know that money doesn't grow on trees, but we're willing to try. "

Lucas, outbidding, launched an even more absurd idea: "Why not go with 'Karter Finance: We've been making finance sexy since 1985'?" It would give a boost to our image!

The room exploded with laughter. There was something liberating about these exchanges, a collective energy that stimulated their creativity and gave them the confidence to face the challenges ahead.

Richard, resuming his serious tone, concludes: "Well, I think we should choose a title that reflects our new beginning and ambition." Something like 'Karter Finance: Emerging a New Era.'

Alex: "Yes, I'll write the article with Lucas." We will create a narrative that will captivate our readers and show them that Karter Finance is ready to cross mountains. And let's not forget that we are preparing for our trip to meet investors in Panama, which will allow us to realize our ambitions.

Tori said: "Let's go then!" I feel this article will create a sensation and restore the image of Karter Finance, and Alex, I would not be in your suitcase for the trip but by your side in your father's most beautiful jet. »

Agent Collins gathered sufficient evidence to launch a major operation in front of the prosecutor. Having seen countless cases, this promised to be among the most complex of his career.

Collins settled in front of him, a thick folder in his hands, filled with documents that might bring down one of the most sophisticated criminal networks in the region.

Collins stated: "Prosecutor, we have overwhelming evidence that links Harris to an extensive money laundering network involving real estate transactions in Greenwood Hills and Florida."

The prosecutor encouraging Collins to continue. The agent placed the file pages on the table as Collins stared at them.

Collins stated: "Our research shows that Harris used several shell companies to purchase and resell land at inflated prices." In particular, he gained plots intended to construe a luxury retirement home and a private airfield, which he named 'Charlie Victor Delta.'

The prosecutor, intrigued by the name, raised an eyebrow. Collins expected his question and continued.

Collins: 'Charlie Victor Delta' derives from the initials of 'curb vis to do' is an anagram of 'Victor Dubois'. We discovered that this Victor Dubois is a pillar of this network, operating from the shadows. It appears that there is a triangle of power between Greenwood Hills, Florida, and an unknown third point, known as the 'Delta'. "

The prosecutor realized the riddle was complex.

"How fascinating," said the prosecutor. "Where do you think this third point is located? "

Collins expressed "uncertainty, but we believe uncovering this third point is crucial to dismantling the network. We suspect that this Victor Dubois, who disappeared from radar screens, is still active and that he is orchestrating these operations from this mysterious location."

Prosecutor asked: "And what about Karter Finance?" Where does he fit into this case? "

Collins adjusted his glasses before answering, choosing his words to avoid undue involvement from Richard Karter.

Collins: "Harris used Karter Finance to manage his investments. Richard Karter, although unaware of Harris' illegal activities, served as a cover for his transactions. However, our evidence shows that Karter Finance treated these funds as regular investments, without suspicion. "

The prosecutor paused, analyzing the legal implications of every detail.

The prosecutor said: "This complicates the situation. We need to ensure that we only direct our accusations at Harris and her network. Please inform me of the next steps."

Collins said: "We have audio recordings that capture Harris fully discussing his plans, and we have witnesses ready to testify, including Harris' phone recording, implicating Inspector Mitchell, who blackmailed Lucas to silence the journalist." I recommend we issue arrest warrants for Harris and his direct accomplices, while ensuring increased surveillance on the other associates for additional evidence."

The prosecutor thinks for a moment, weighing the pros and cons.

The prosecutor said, "You have the green light."

Collins: "Thank you, Mr. Prosecutor. We are going to name this operation "Operation Shadow Hunt."

The operation was in progress, and he knew it would enhance the agency's reputation and the justice system.

The atmosphere was that of meet family and allies, each aware of the path traveled and the road that opened up in front of them. Richard, sitting with an imposing posture, showed satisfaction, his eyes twinkling with a pride he did not hide. Tori, in an elegant dress, was overflowing with enthusiasm, her place within the Karter family finally assured. Lucas, released, was beaming with obvious relief, aware of the second chance he had received.

Alex spoke, his gaze passing over every face around the table:

"The article is a success," he said, tapping the newspaper in front of him. "This is what we needed to restore our image and show that Karter Finance is back, stronger than ever."

Richard: "It's a masterstroke, Alex. With this article, we have done more than restore our reputation; we have set a new standard."

Tori, unable to contain her joy, added: "It's thanks to the collective effort of each of us. And Lucas, your article lived up to expectations. Congratulations!"

Lucas raised his glass: "Thank you, Tori. I am honored to be part of this journey with all of you."

They took a moment to enjoy lunch, bursts of laughter punctuating the conversation. Then Tori turned to Richard with an amusing suggestion. "Mr. Richard Karter, perhaps you could consider a career in politics after all this. You already have the speech for!"

Richard burst out laughing, shaking his head. "No, thank you, Tori. Politics is much more complicated than finance, and I prefer the challenges that I know."

Lucas intervened, a mischievous smile on his lips:

"We could also launch a title contest for the next articles. I propose 'Karter Finance: Finances and Festivities'."

Everyone burst out laughing, the atmosphere becoming lighter. Alex took advantage of this moment of relaxation to relax and enjoy the shared camaraderie.

Alex's assistant entered, carrying a tablet with the latest news: "Mr. Karter, the engagement figures following the article are already impressive. Social networks are ablaze with positive comments."

Tori: "It means that our strategy is working. We have to maintain this momentum."

They launched Operation Shadow Hunt. The long-awaited moment had arrived to strike at the heart of Harris's criminal network.

Agent Collins was coordinating the operation. The teams were about to leave: "Today we are dismantling Harris's empire," announced Collins.

The FBI vehicles deployed in the city. The primary target was Harris's sumptuous residence, a place that has become a symbol of his criminal arrogance. While the cars were sliding through the streets, each team rehearsed the plan, elaborated with meticulousness.

In front of Harris' villa, the agents are making progress. The trimmed hedges saw them in the blink of an eye. They entered the property, making sure that every movement was silent and calculated.

In the dining room of the residence, Harris was enjoying his morning coffee, surrounded by his wife. His nonchalance contrasted with the tension outside.the distinct sound of doors opening on the fly startled him.

"FBI! Don't move! "The voice of Agent Collins burst into the room, imposing and irrefutable."

Harris raised his hands, his smile smirking:

"Do you think you've set me up? "He tried to escape, but the agents' determination left no room for him to do so."

Meanwhile, at the other end of the city, a special team approached Inspector Mitchell, who had faced compromise in the case. For weeks, was under surveillance. As he was about to leave for headquarters, convinced that he was still above suspicion, his colleagues intercepted him.

"Detective Mitchell, you are under arrest for suspicion of complicity with a criminal organization," Officer Taylor said.

Surprised, Mitchell allowed himself to be handcuffed, his face frozen by amazement and incomprehension. "How could you... He stammered.

With the capture of Harris and Mitchell, the Shadow Hunt operation had succeeded beyond expectations. The head of the criminal network that had plagued Greenwood Hills was disintegrating under the effect of the arrests. Federal agents escorted the suspects to the waiting vehicles.

Alex's assistant knocked on the door to attract her bosses.the hubbub of the discussions faded away, and all eyes turned to her, a silent expectation in the air.

"I am sorry to interrupt you," she began, "but I have news to tell you." She paused, letting the suspense settle in. "The news I have to tell you is the FBI arrested that Harris," she began, interrupting.

Alex stood up straight, a slight smile of satisfaction stretching his lips. He turned his head to Richard, his father. This arrest was not just a victory, but a crucial step towards the rehabilitation and stabilization of Karter Finance.

Richard, with a smile imbued with sincere gratitude, addressed the assembly: "This deserves a celebration. This victory shows that we are on the right track to straighten out our image."

The room burst into a collective murmur of joy and relief. The tense faces relaxed, and optimism infused the atmosphere like a subtle but powerful perfume.

Alex, however, could not repress a thought that haunted him. With his hands folded in front of him, he asked a question that weighed on his mind:

"Is Harris the killer of Eleanor and my friend?"

"There is no information on this point at the moment, Mr. Karter. They will talk about it on GWTV5."

Richard takes the remote control of his large suspended TV. The small Karter committee is waiting to follow the information.

Alex launches text exchanges with Lucas and Daniel, also thanks Agent Collins.

CHAPTER 9

OPERATION CHARLIE VICTOR DELTA

The Karter company, run by Richard and his son Alex, was once again in full expansion. Richard discovered a new asset, Tori. He saw in her the ideal daughter, a feminine presence that would enhance the Karter family's image. Not all large families comprise many children or grandchildren, and those that are sometimes torn over inheritance issues or dispersed.

Today, at the Karter Finance headquarters, the team focused their attention on the Panama City project. Since the financial crisis, the company had experienced remarkable growth but external turbulence, independent of the markets, had arisen. Wise Richard, as the patriarch, expected and defused them.

Today, we are going to plant our flag with the letter "K" in Panama City. "Millions will pour into our coffers," declared Richard in a hoarse voice, filled with determination.

Alex, standing next to his father, spoke up:

"Our solid financial base now allows us to get ahead of our competitors and strengthen our credibility with our new investors. Recent events must remind us that vigilance in our family affairs is more crucial than ever."

"Well spoken, my son," retorted Richard with pride.

"Thanks, dad," Alex replied, before turning to Tori. "Let's take an example from Tori. Despite the pain of losing her mother, she got back up and was part of our adventure. Welcome to our family, Tori."

A few discreet applause emanated from the members of the council, marking their approval. Tori knew that her network of contacts in Panama would be decisive in establishing the essential connections.

We must approach every interaction with my contacts with openness. "Their conditions are optimal and allow us to penetrate the Panamanian market," she says.

"Peace to his soul," Richard whispered. "From above, he must be proud of his daughter-in-law. The Greenwood Hills Journal article was a first step to restore our coat of arms. You and Alex will soon multiply our investment by ten. The lovebirds are taking flight this week!"

The board's faces reflected relief. The accountant, who adjusted his tie to show that the accounts were in balance.

After a two-hour meeting punctuated by questions and answers, the three pillars of Karter Finance found themselves alone to complete the documents and contracts.

It was past 13 o'clock when Richard, late for a scheduled lunch with his wife Margaret, arrived. The embraces were quick, almost mechanical, like a ritual performed out of habit.

Margaret, a woman who had navigated the twists and turns of life alongside a business tycoon, possessed a sharp intelligence and a deep understanding of the issues that surrounded them. She had learned to forgive Richard's absences, understanding that every moment stolen from their relationship was often the price of their success.

Richard knew Margaret was not only a wife but also Alex's mother, his greatest pride. She understood the strategic implications of every decision and had always balanced grace and insight.

Margaret, you're the first to know. Alex is leaving for Panama City. Establishing Karter Finance there has become a priority," he announced.

Margaret smiled. "Panama, you say? I knew this day would come. You're always one step ahead, Richard."

Richard felt a silent pride. He had this rare ability to turn every challenge into an opportunity. He bowed towards her, as if to share a secret.

"I think it's also an opportunity to talk about our commitments. How is your project progressing with the parish? A well-orchestrated communication about your efforts could do wonders for our image."

"My project is progressing well. We have involved the community. And you're right, it's time to make it known."

She saw this trip to Panama as an opportunity to strengthen the couple's foundations. She knew that the balance of their lives was fragile since the scandal with Jim. It was essential to maintain an impeccable image. Their union, built on trust and shared ambition, could overcome the betrayals that had left deep scars.

The revelations resulting from interrogating Harris had opened up new perspectives in the investigation, highlighting crucial information.

During the search of the Harris Airfield, the agents had discovered unexpected elements. An ordinary hangar housed a small passenger plane used for illicit operations. The device bore the traces of regular activity, with fingerprints taken on the dashboard, the joysticks and the seats, suggesting frequent use.

After analysis, these prints corresponded to those of Mr. Blackwood, alias "Victor Dubois", a well-known name in the FBI. This man had operated in the shadows for years, orchestrating large-scale operations while escaping justice. His sudden disappearance from the radars perplexed investigators, but now they have a solid lead. Dubois had taken advantage of his escape to escape those who were trying to make him disappear.

Taylor, the team leader's assistant, continued:

"Dubois used Harris Airfield as a transit point. His expertise as a pilot allowed him to navigate between jurisdictions, complicating his location and arrest. We also discovered that the aircraft used for these operations made frequent stops in Florida, strengthening the link with other ongoing investigations."

The documents found at the airfield did not show a direct link between Dubois and Karter Finance, but he had infiltrated the company through third parties and subtle manipulations orchestrated by Harris. Tori, his daughter, seemed to play a key role in this plot. Her presence within Karter Finance was not the result of the chance her father had placed there with her to facilitate his operations under the guise of respectability.

The FBI knew it had to act and. Operation Charlie Victor Delta, named after the enigmatic triangular network connecting Dubois to his activities in Greenwood Hills, Florida, and soon in Panama, had the aim of stopping him.

The FBI's strategy was straightforward: leverage the evidence to force Harris into full cooperation, all the while planning to intercept Alex's jet as it headed towards Panama. The aim was to secure the suitcase containing the funds, but also to follow the trail that would lead to Dubois.

Mr. Blackwood's past added a layer of complexity to the investigation. Dubois, a former fighter and experienced pilot, had used his skills to eliminate those who stood in his way. His fingerprints found on Harris' plane confirmed his role.

Inside a deserted aviation hangar, a heavy atmosphere prevailed. Inside a deserted aviation hangar, a heavy atmosphere prevailed, with the carcasses of abandoned fuselages scattered about like wounded birds. These carcasses concealed the secret activities taking place here, with tall trees as tall as the control tower providing additional cover. Because of its discretion, away from prying eyes, the FBI selected this location for the briefing.

Amended: Permeating the air, the humidity entered through the ajar panoramic door, supported by rusted beams. In the center of the space, a large table covered with a plastic and folders marked "Top Secret" occupied attending Agents Collins and Taylor. They were finishing installing a computer, preparing for the final stages of the briefing.

Alex Karter sneaked through, opening the door marked by the place. The propellers of the old parked planes still imposed a silent and threatening presence.

"Thank you for coming, Mr. Karter," Collins said, greeting him. "Don't worry, we won't use these remains to travel."

"It must be important and confidential to justify an appointment here," Alex replied, on his guard.

Collins opened a large folder, revealing photographs and analysis reports. "We found decisive evidence after arresting Harris and searching his airfield."

"Mr. Blackwood? You mean Eleanor's husband?" asked Alex.

"Yes, and Tori Blackwood's father," Collins added.

Taylor spoke up: "Dubois is not just a pawn. He is the mastermind behind a criminal organization of an unsuspected scale. He seems to have used his aeronautical expertise to facilitate illegal transits."

Tori's silence gnawed at Alex. But even more, the idea of his father being manipulated without his knowledge disconcerted him.

"What about Tori in all this? Was she an accomplice or just trapped by her father?" Alex wondered, divided between anger and confusion.

"We believe Tori has maintained close ties with her father. It's possible that she later found out that he was still alive, but for reasons that are still unclear, she said nothing," Collins explained. "For now, these are only assumptions. We have put surveillance in place."

Alex felt a distrust rise in him dictated by his instinct. He began to "switch" his feelings for her, a growing distrust replacing trust.

Taylor continued, "We also consider that Dubois could have a link to the murders of Madame Blackwood and other key figures."

"How did it happen that Tori's father became a killer? And if he did indeed commit Eleanor's murder, it is abominable!" exclaimed Alex, horrified by this prospect.

Collins intervened: "Our plan is simple, but it could expose you to dangers, Mr. Karter we know you have to go to Panama, during your flight to Panama, we will intercept the jet on board one of our aircraft carrier ships to check the contents of the suitcase handed over by your father. We must secure all potential evidence. Are you going to transfer cash, Mr. Karter?"

"Indeed, my father is going to make a transfer of funds, and among this enormous sum, there is also Tori's money," Alex confirmed.

"With the help of our on-board services, we will replace the real tickets with fake ones, in order to bring out the "bottom mud". Are you following me this far?" Collins asked, scrutinizing Alex's reaction.

"We ask you to remain vigilant and to keep absolute discretion, even in front of Tori. Count on us to ensure the safety and integrity of this mission. "As soon as you arrive," Collins concludes, "we will station agents on-site."

The morning had risen over the Karter residence, bathing the rooms in a discreet clarity. Yet an imperceptible tension permeated the air.the day to depart for Panama City had arrived, increasing our anticipation with each passing moment.

Alex had slept. The revelations of the FBI, still fresh in his mind, continued to obsess him since the secret briefing. He descended the steps, the light sound of his footsteps on the parquet floor in no way disturbing the tranquility of the house. The thick curtains let through a perceptible burst of light, insufficient to dissipate the morning shadow that still reigned in the house.

Arranged near the door, the luggage marked beginning this special day. Alex stopped in front of the suitcases, his gaze resting on the most imposing one, the one that contained much more than just belongings; it symbolized the responsibility that now weighed on his shoulders.

He then headed for the kitchen, hoping to find a distraction in the familiar gestures of making coffee. The murmur of the coffee pot broke the silence, but it brought no comfort. Hangar images, federal agent instructions, all looped back, plunging him into uninterrupted reflection.

Richard entered at that moment, displaying a disconcerting calm. Unlike his son, he seemed a stranger to worry. His gaze, lively, was this time imbued with a serenity that upset Alex's nervousness?

"Did you sleep well? "Richard asked, breaking a clear tranquility.

Alex, despite his restless mind, replied with an affirmative nod, thus hiding the exhaustion that inhabited him. He knew he had to appear assured, so as not to arouse suspicions. Richard, confident as always, seemed unaware of the risks Alex faced. This quiet certainty that he displayed became, for his son, both a comfort and a pressure.

"I'm finally going to stay here a little longer," Richard declared. An urgent matter requires my attention. You two leave without me. I will meet you in Panama City as soon as possible. »

These words had an immediate impact on Alex. Richard's absence added an extra layer of complexity to an already perilous mission. He realized that the responsibilities that awaited him in Panama were taking on an extra dimension, a gravity that he had not expected.

"Okay," Alex replied, in a controlled voice. He could not afford to show the trouble that inhabited him. Henceforth, success in this operation relied on him, without his father's direct support.

Tori joined them after, dressed for the trip, her dynamism sharp with the tense atmosphere. She greeted Richard's decision with silent acceptance. "You will join us soon, won't you? "She asked.

"As soon as possible. I trust you for this first step," Richard affirmed.

The morning passed as everyone prepared for what lay ahead. Alex was trying to maintain his composure, preparing himself for this new dynamic. He longed for Tori's undivided attention and understanding. He had to remain impassive.

The time of departure arrived. Richard stood by the door, watching Alex and Tori as they loaded the suitcases into the car. His piercing stare bore into his son's soul, desperate to uncover what lay beneath.

"Have a pleasant trip," Richard said, putting a firm hand on Alex's shoulder. "Take care of her and the company."

Alex replied with a slight movement of his head, his thoughts too cluttered to plan an adequate answer. The stakes of the mission, the absence of his father, the need to remain vigilant in front of Tori... all this weighed, but he had to hide it, at least until they arrived in Panama.

Richard waved to them one last time as the car pulled away. Alex, glancing in the rear-view mirror, saw his father's figure fading into the distance. He transformed from being a mere son to the one tasked with a risky operation that could change their destiny.

The atmosphere in the car was dense, almost suffocating, while the landscapes scrolled by, each kilometer bringing them closer to their destination and the challenges ahead. Alex remained focused on the road, his thoughts plagued by a whirlwind of scenarios, aware of the uncertainties that awaited them in Panama City.

Arriving on the tarmac of the private airport, Alex and Tori's footsteps echoed, their silhouettes standing out in the subtle morning light. A light breeze was raising swirls of dust, adding to the already tense atmosphere. Around the jet, the airport staff was busy in silence, making sure that everything was ready for a crucial flight.

Tori was moving forward with a resolute step, her backpack snug on her shoulders. An intense concentration marked his face, almost unrecognizable. Alex, meanwhile, struggled to contain his restless thoughts, each step stressing the weight of his responsibilities. In his right hand he held a leather suitcase, heavy not only with its contents but also with the expectations it represented. This suitcase embodied the hopes and the risks inherent in their mission.

"I never thought that a financial mission could be akin to a clandestine operation," Tori observed, breaking the silence between them. His voice, light, this time, carried a new depth.

Alex tried to answer with a reassuring smile. "Business can sometimes feel like battles," he replied. Be prepared for anything once we arrive.

They reached the staircase leading to the jet's entrance. An airport agent, dressed with care, greeted them, confirming that everything was in order for their departure. Alex replied with a slight nod, his thoughts focused on the suitcase he was carrying, aware of what it contained. Before boarding, he memorized the familiar landscape, taking one last look.

As she walked up the steps, Tori turned to Alex, her expression marked by a gravity that he had never seen in her home. "Alex, I understand prizing this trip for Karter Finance, but for me, it is also an opportunity to show what I am capable of. I am ready to do whatever is necessary for us to succeed."

Alex's words held determination, yet he remained burdened by secrets. "I am certain that we will succeed together, Tori," he said, gripping the handle of the suitcase before entering the cabin of the jet at his side.

The interior of the jet, designed for comfort and elegance, was in marked contrast to the concerns that invaded Alex's mind. Soft leather seats, generous space, and high-end equipment created a balanced world, despite the distant reality. Alex put the suitcase at his feet, feeling its symbolic weight at every moment as a constant reminder of the mission that awaited them.

As the plane rolled on the runway, Alex settled down near a porthole, his gaze lost in the landscape that was drifting away. Each meter traveled took them a little further away from Greenwood Hills, plunging them into a future with blurred outlines. But he knew he had to stay focused and keep his composure.

Tori, sitting next to him, seemed immersed in her reflections, going over the various scenarios for their mission. The silence between them carried a palpable intensity, filled with unspoken questions that might take a while to be answered.

During takeoff, Alex experienced a rare mix of aloneness and connection with Tori. This trip, he knew, was going to mark a turning point. Each decision, every step, carried consequences, all traced back to this deceptive suitcase.

The private jet was speeding through the immensity of the ocean, its engines purring in the hushed calm of the cabin. Alex, sitting by the porthole, was watching the waves below, his mind occupied with the operation in progress and the precise instructions he had received from Collins. Tori, installed near to him, was browsing through documents on her phone, focused on the preparations for the upcoming appointments in Panama City, without suspecting what was happening.

A slight jolt made the device shudder. The pilot's voice sounds: "Mr. Karter, Mrs. Blackwood, we have received authorization to make an emergency landing on an aircraft carrier for refueling. This landing will be tricky. "

Tori, raising her head from her phone:

"An aircraft carrier? It's unusual, isn't it? "

Alex nodded, trying to keep a reassuring tone:

"This is an emergency protocol. The pilot knows what he's doing. "

Through the porthole, the aircraft carrier appeared, an imposing silhouette on the waves. Alex's stomach twisted with anguish at the idea of landing a private jet designed for much longer runways in the ocean's vastness, making the ship seem tiny in comparison.

With a more tense voice, the pilot warns them:

"Hang on. It will be a challenging landing. No other choice, despite the jet's unsuitability for this maneuver. "

Alex exchanged a glance with Tori, who clutched the armrests of her seat. The stress was visible on her face, but she remained silent, her pursed lips reflecting an anxiety that she was struggling to mask.

The approach to the aircraft carrier was meticulous, each movement of the jet measured to avoid disaster. Each change in altitude felt like a heart leap to both passengers. As the jet descended, the ship's deck grew in sight, but it still seemed much too short for a safe landing.

"Be careful of the impact," announced the pilot in a tense voice. The aircraft descended in a dive, then the landing gear touched the deck of the aircraft carrier with a sharp shock. The thud of the impact echoed through the cabin, followed by a shrill screech of tires struggling to find their grip on the metal surface.

Despite their seat belts, the shaking jet threw Alex and Tori against their seats. Their bodies tensed under the effort, as the pilot fought to keep the aircraft in a straight line. The jet skids before the pilot straightens its trajectory.

"Is everything fine?" Tori asked, her voice betraying genuine panic for the first time.

Alex, breathless from the tension, whispers, "It's going to be okay." Stay calm.

The jet continues to slow down, the aircraft carrier's restraint cables straining under the force of the aircraft. After what felt like forever, the jet stopped, its engines making one last roar before shutting off.

A heavy silence fell on the cabin, disturbed only by the hum of the aircraft's systems. Alex and Tori paused.

The pilot speaking again:

"Landing completed. A sense of security surrounded us, enabling us to finally breathe easy. Please stay on board while refueling is in progress."

Alex releases his grip on the armrests, the joints whitened by the force of his grip. He turned his head to Tori, who was breathing, trying to regain her composure.

"It was... more than delicate," whispered Tori

"Yes," he said, trying to control his own breathing. "But here we are. "

While the crew of the aircraft carrier was busy around the jet, simulating refueling, Alex got up, his mind still troubled by the perilous maneuver they had just experienced. "I'm going to make sure everything is in order," he said, maintaining a neutral tone despite the adrenaline that was still pounding in his veins.

Tori nodded without answering, still in shock from the landing. Alex left the cabin.

Outside, an FBI agent disguised as a crew member was waiting for him. "Mr. Karter, this way, please," he said with a discretion tinged with urgency. The exchange had to be done without arousing Tori's suspicions. The recent event's shadow loomed over Alex, fueling his determination for a flawless outcome.

They descended a narrow ramp leading to the depths of the ship. The air inside was cool, contrasting with the overwhelming heat of the bridge. The aircraft carrier dampened the sounds, creating an almost unreal atmosphere. Two agents in a small room waited with an open briefcase.

"We have to move," said one agent while getting down to the task. They exchanged the contents of the suitcase, replacing the real money with fake banknotes. Each movement precise, notes crumpling, echoing in tense silence.

Alex watched them in silence. This exchange was just one decisive step. Once the briefcase was closed and handed to Alex, the senior agent looked him straight in the eye. You're running out of time before we go act.

He gets back on board the jet. He finds Tori still focused on her preparations. "All set," he reassured, resuming his seat.

After refueling was complete, the jet restarted its full-throttle engines to resume its flight to

Panama City. The sky stretched out in front of them again, while the aircraft carrier disappeared from their field of vision.

Tori, focused on preparations, remained oblivious to the recent operation before her. While Alex prepared for what awaited them, the jet continued its journey with deceptive tranquility. Soon, the hour of revelations would arrive, bringing them closer to when everything would change.

The dense and oppressive air of Panama City seizes them as soon as they leave Tocumen Airport. Alex and Tori navigated the crowd, an agent amidst confusion. The city was a veritable whirlwind of activities. Spanish voices and street tumult destabilized Alex.

The towers of the financial district rose like modern fortresses. These massive buildings dominate an urban landscape that contrasted with the surrounding historic districts. On the horizon, the hills offered a natural backdrop to this metropolis, recalling the coexistence of nature and the city.

Tori, at ease in this dynamic environment, continued her exchanges in Spanish with their local contacts. Alex, although despite an effort for this language learned at his university, tried to read the innuendos in the expressions and reactions of those around them.

They got into a discreet car sent by their hotel, which led them through the busy avenues of the city. The skyscrapers of the center gave way to old buildings. In the Casco Viejo district, you'll find cobbled streets and colorful facades.

Located in the heart of the financial district, the hotel where they arrived provided a luxurious sanctuary.

Dropping off his suitcase in their suite, Alex looked around the room, stopping for a moment on a man whose attitude aroused his distrust. This observation confirms his impression that someone noticed their arrival. The FBI, so far in retreat, could well enter the scene sooner than expected.

After dark, Alex stood by the window, contemplating the city lights that dotted the night sky. The suitcase, placed at his side, also marks a time of pause.

The next day, Alex and Tori were walking with a decided step, ready to meet Tori's contacts. They entered a discreet building, where the welcome was brief and formal. Tori took charge of the discussion, exchanging in Spanish with the intermediaries in an assured tone. Alex, who did not understand everything, tried to capture the essentials by examining the faces of the interlocutors.

Time passed, and the conversation became more tense. One intermediary, whose gaze hardened, asked questions that put Tori on the defensive. Alex felt a growing discomfort, a dull concern invading him as the situation seemed to escape him.

The door opened, and Richard entered, late but determined. He took his seat, listening to Tori's explanation. Although Richard sought to restore appear calm, the distrust of the intermediaries was becoming more and more visible. The exchanges continued, but the atmosphere was now electric.

The intermediary requested to see the money. Tori, without hesitation, unlocked the suitcase and pushed it onto the table. The man examined the notes with particular attention, his features closing as he continued his inspection. When he realized the notes were fake, his gaze darkened more. Tori, surprised, her eyes searching for answers from Alex and Richard. After a quick exchange in Spanish with his colleagues, anger erupted. The accusations burst out; the voices rising. Alex, although not grasping at everything, understood that the situation was deteriorating.

The tension culminated when one man, at his wits' end, pulled out a gun and pointed it at Richard. The latter raised his hands, trying to defuse the confrontation. Seeing no other way out, Richard pulled out a pistol, ready to defend himself. Chaos erupted in the room, voices shifting to screams, shots fired, notes fluttering amidst the chaos.

Tori, reacting, grabbed the suitcase and rushed to the exit. The bullets whistled around her, but she fought her way through the fray. For his part, Alex, far from remaining paralyzed, jumped forward. He threw himself on one of the armed men, engaging in a fierce struggle to disarm the attacker. The sound of blows and bodies colliding added to the general confusion.

Richard, while trying to contain the shooting, glanced at Alex, who was fighting with fierce determination. The situation was out of control, but his son's courage gave him a boost of strength to hold his position.

Meanwhile, Tori was running, determined to put as much distance between herself and the scene of the shooting as possible. Every step brought her closer to the meeting point. Her phone vibrated, and she picked up, answering in a breathless voice in Spanish:

"Estoy en camino. (I'm on my way.)

She continued her race. With the help of her lighter blew up the car in front of the entrance, her telephone exchanges revealed her true allegiance.

The agents stationed in the streets take it in, spinning without being noticed

Tori arrived at the meeting place, a remote warehouse, away from prying eyes. His breath was still quick after his hasty flight. Inside she found her father, Mr. Blackwood, waiting for her with a visible expression of impatience. Despite years in hiding, he maintained an imposing assurance, typical of one accustomed to controlling all situations.

Tori handed the suitcase to her father, looking for some form of comfort in his gaze. Mr. Blackwood opened the suitcase, looked at it, but his face hardened as he discovered the truth.

"What is this? "He asked, anger piercing his voice.

Tori, taken aback, realized what she had missed in the shooting's confusion:

"These are fake banknotes... "She whispered, her voice filled with a mixture of disbelief and panic. She had focused too much on their escape to realize the deception earlier.

Mr. Blackwood closed his eyes for a moment, controlling the anger that was bubbling inside him. "How could this have happened?

" He snarled, straightened up, and his mind was already searching for a solution."

Tori, feeling the situation slipping away from them, moved closer to her father, hoping that he would find a way out of this trap. Mr. Blackwood thought, reviewing the options they had left.

"We must reverse this situation," he muttered, addressing Tori and himself. He was planning a plan when powerful headlights invaded the warehouse, illuminating every corner and casting ominous shadows on the walls. In a split second, the roar of several unmarked vehicles that surrounded the building broke the calm.

Tori felt her heart racing, a growing panic invading her. Plainclothes agents appeared on all sides, weapons in hand, their movements precise and determined. Mr. Blackwood stiffened, understanding that the situation had just swung out of their control.

"FBI! Don't move! "Shouted one of the leading agents. His voice echoed in the warehouse." The sound of weapons ready to fire echoed in the air, arguing more palpable than ever.

Tori, unsettled by the sudden turn of events, turned her gaze to her father. Despite feeling dissatisfied with the way things were unfolding, Mr. Blackwood acknowledged that they were trapped. A glimmer of resignation passed in his eyes. He understood their time was running out and luck had changed.

"Dad, there must be another solution..." she whispered, her voice broken by urgency and fear.

Mr. Blackwood, always calculating, tried to ignore the surrounding chaos to evaluate their options. But before he could sketch out an answer, the FBI agents had already stepped forward, their embrace tightening around the fugitives.

"It's over, Tori," he said, his words heavy with meaning.he raised his hands in surrender, aware that they no longer had an escape. With regret in his eyes, he looked at his daughter in a timeless silence.

"Tori... I'm sorry about your mom. And for the money, you have yours. That money, I remind you, was mine. It could have been a delicate operation to clear me one last time. Her voice, usually so confident, was filled with sadness and disillusionment. This simple admission, loaded with guilt and regret, was like a stab for Tori, who stared at him with wide eyes, her world collapsing around her.

The shock of this revelation, added to the desperate situation in which they found themselves, left her speechless. Everything she had thought she understood about their relationship, their history, was wavering under the weight of this admission.

The agents approached, breaking this heartbreaking moment of intimacy. One of them handcuffed Tori, and despite her desire to flee, she let herself go, still stunned by her father's words. Mr. Blackwood's gaze remained fixed on her, revealing his frustration, disappointment, and sadness.

The chief of the agents, advancing with a firm step, stared at Mr. Blackwood. "Mr. Blackwood, Tori Blackwood, you are under arrest."

Mr. Blackwood, still stoic, turned to Tori one last time. "Don't worry. They won't do you any harm. They want me. "Tori, her thoughts spinning at full speed, could not bring herself to accept this end. She frantically searched for a way out, rejecting the idea that everything was lost.

FBI vehicles transported fugitives while the warehouse regained silence, disturbed by red and blue warning lights' reflections. Car doors closed, secrets taken, leaving desolation.

And while intervention vehicles, taking Tori and her father to an outcome that will judge them up to their deeds.

Operation Charlie Victor Delta is a success.

How would Alex and Richard fare in a case that surpassed their abilities?

CHAPTER 10

REDEMPTION IN GREENWOOD HILLS

In the mansion, a strange calm filled the air. Alex stood by the stairs, eyes fixed on the floor, trying to comprehend the sudden alienation of this once vibrant place. Something intangible had changed, not just in the walls, but also within him. The familiar earth's warmth felt distant to him now.

Richard, a few steps away, was observing the room with attention, his features marked by fatigue. He wandered the hall, seeking a connection to their long-standing sanctuary.

Margaret, standing in the living room, she was trying to catch the silent thoughts of her loved ones. She understood those moments when everyone sought balance.

"Take a moment to ask yourself, "she finally said, her voice soft but resolute.

Dinner awaits you in the dining room. You will need to regain your strength for what will follow. "

Richard headed for the dining room. He dabbed the family photo on the console as a reminder of his duty to protect. The fleeting contact with the polished wood reminded him of a simpler time.

Alex followed his father, his heavy footsteps echoing faintly on the parquet floor, his heart still in the throes of a restlessness that he could not calm down.

They discovered the table already set, the plates delicately aligned, the glasses shining under the dim light of the chandelier. Margaret joined them, settling down with natural elegance, finally spoke:

"What you experienced there... "She began, but her words hung in the air."

I can't fathom the experience. We need this moment to refocus.

Richard listened in silence.

"That's right. We cannot afford to let what has happened bring us down. This mansion, this family, that's all we have. And we protect that, no matter what it costs. "

His voice, although firm, was a fatigue that went beyond simple physical exhaustion.

Alex raised his head, searching his mother's eyes before speaking. "Nothing here seems the same anymore. It's as if... He paused, searching for the right words to articulate his emotions. Everything has changed, not just because of what happened. "

"This mansion, this house, it's what we do with it now that matters. We must remember why we are here, together. And this we must protect. "She whispered," she said.

She paused, looking at Richard and Alex.

"I think it's time to forget about the past tragedies. We can overcome all this if we choose to focus on the future. Let's focus on what we have and what we can build. It's time to start again on new efforts, but differently, considering everything we have learned. "

Silence fell on the table again. They all silently acknowledged what they had to confront.

That evening, the mansion seemed less cold, less distant. He was a home again. Richard, facing his own cogitations, makes a monologue. Alone in the library late, he smokes a cigar while the rooms sleep. The silent news screen illuminates his silhouette. Her loneliness helps her to question herself like a rehearsal before going back on stage. What is he up to?

The night will restore for a new day.

At Karter Finance, an unusual atmosphere reigned that morning.

The room was silent, everyone sensing an extraordinary meeting.

This meeting also surprised Richard's beloved son, but really feels like he has been since their return.

Richard Karter, at the room's center, appeared unlike his confident self. His gestures were slower. He looked at each executive, then focused on his son.

"Thank you for coming this morning," Richard began, his voice calm.

A careful silence set in as the council members prepared to hear what their leader had to say.

Recent events have been challenging for both the company and each individual. Allow me to share my vision for Karter Finance and myself. "

Alex feels a new sensation in front of this man, whom he had always seen as unbeatable. Something profound was about to be revealed.

"I have devoted my life to building this business," Richard continued, his eyes moving from one face to the other with unusual gravity.

"But today I feel the need to turn to something else. Recent challenges made me realize I can make a difference in another area, serving our community. "

A murmur ran through the room as the executives exchanged incredulous glances. Richard Karter, the mainstay of Karter Finance, spoke as if he was considering walking away from the company. His son, meanwhile, feeling that his father's words were about to change not only his life.

"With a solemnity that silenced the slightest whisper, Richard announced his decision to retire gradually from the day-to-day management of Karter Finance."

"Alex," he said, turning to his son, "I wish for you to take over the management of the company." I know you are ready for this challenge. "

The silence that followed this statement was fraught with significance. For Alex, it was an unexpected announcement, a responsibility that he had not expected so soon. But when he met his father's gaze, he understood Richard had considered this decision.

"I'm not retiring completely," Richard continued, "but I think it's time for me to invest differently, to contribute to the future of this city differently. Lead Karter Finance with my same determination and vision. "

Signaling the era's end and a fresh start. Alex felt an excitement arise in him.

Richard then approached, placing a reassuring hand on his son's shoulder. "You have everything you need to succeed, Alex. I know this. "

"I will do everything in my power, Father. Company, you, family. "answers him in a very mature tone.

Richard and Alex ended up in the office, a space that has witnessed countless strategic decisions. The place, typically serene, now felt burdened by impending events. Richard took a seat in his armchair, letting his thoughts wander for a moment, while Alex, still standing, looked at him with increased attention.

"Alex" Richard began, his voice tinged with a rare sweetness." I know this announcement surprised you, and I understand how you may feel. Understand, this decision has been long matured. "

Alex watched his father, trying to read beyond the words. "You have always shown unwavering attachment to this business," he replied, carefully weighing his words. "But lately, I have perceived in you a desire for change. "

Richard confirming his son's words.

"Recent events have changed my perspective," he said. I realized my role here isn't the only place I can make a difference. Our city needs a new lease on life, and I feel ready to devote all my energy to it. "

Alex, absorbed by his father's words, felt a mixture of pride and responsibility knotting in him.

"I understand better now," he said in a low voice. If you believe this is the right path, I'll respect your decision. "

A slight smile appeared on Richard's lips, a smile imbued with gratitude.

"It's a new adventure that begins for both of us, Alex. I'm running for re-election in Greenwood Hills, and I know you'll be up to running Karter Finance. "

Alex: "I will do everything to ensure that this company continues to prosper and reflect the values that you have always instilled in it. I support your political project, I congratulate you. "

Richard then got up, bypassing his desk to stand near his son.

"We are both at the dawn of a new chapter," he said

Alex said, "It's a new beginning."

Richard held out his hand to her, thus sealing their tacit agreement. "Yes, a new beginning, Alex. I am convinced of our individual success, but always together. "

Alex shook his father's hand, a firm grip full of promise. "Together, father. We are always together."

A knock on the office door. The assistant discreetly announces the arrival of the FBI agents.

The FBI agents, installed opposite Richard and Alex, closed this case.

Collins said, "Mr. Karter, we are returning these funds to you," he announced. "The evidence we have collected allows us to put an end to this investigation. "

Richard welcomed this news with controlled calmness. "Thank you, gentlemen. It is a relief to see this case finally resolved. "

Collins: "We would also like to thank you, Alex, for your cooperation. Your help has been essential in moving this investigation forward and reaching its conclusion. "

Alex: "I simply did what was necessary." It was important to discover the truth and ensure justice. "

Collins: "Without your commitment, things could have taken a much different direction. We are grateful for your support. "

Richard, listening to these exchanges, felt a discreet pride for his son.

"Alex has always done what was necessary," he added with a restrained warmth in his voice.

Collins: "We must also inform you that Tori Blackwood is in custody. The property she inherited will be put up for auction soon for her deposit. Given the circumstances, this measure was necessary. "

Richard paused to process the information, a brief expression of relief crossing his face.

"It's reassuring to know that this situation is finally being resolved "

Alex, however, remained concerned about the future implications. What consequences might Karter Finance face? "He asked, his tone serious, while trying to gauge the potential repercussions."

Collins: "To date, there is nothing to show a direct threat to your company. However, it remains prudent to remain vigilant in the future. "

Alex affirmed, "We will be on our guard," determined to protect the interests of his family and the company.

Richard, perceiving his son's persistent concern, put a comforting hand on his arm.

"Alex, we have overcome many trials," he said confidently. "This one is no exception. It's time to turn the page and focus on the future. "

Despite his father's soothing words, Alex remained aware of the challenges ahead.

"Yes, father," he replied, ready to face whatever might yet arise.

The agents, deeming their mission accomplished, rose to take their leave. "Thank you again for your cooperation," one of them said, shaking Alex's hand. "If other elements should appear, we would inform you immediately. In the meantime, be careful. "

The men leave the camp, leaving this suitcase full of cash.

Richard walking to the window, his thought oscillating between relief and caution.

"We've been through this storm," he whispered. "You are the captain now. "

Alex: "Dad, do you know what I'm seeing? "looking at the suitcase on the table

Richard: "No, my son,"

Alex stretches out his arm pointing his fingers towards the suitcase. "I see a beautiful political campaign for you right in front! "

Richard: "Holy Alex, you are indeed your father's son! "her face gives off a radiant smile.

The two friends organize a lunch, taking advantage of the mild weather.

The restaurant's terrace, perched on a hill, dominated the city with a breathtaking view of the hills. Reflecting an era of elegance and minimalism, the place was a precious relic. It featured wooden balusters and delicate wrought iron lanterns. The soft light of lunch created the warm and serene atmosphere, ideal for reunions with friends flooding the space.

Alex and Lucas sat near the edge, where the panorama was spectacular.

"I love this place," Lucas said, observing the surrounding details. "It's like we've jumped back in time. "

Alex: "I thought this was the perfect place to tell you everything that's happened recently. "

Lucas, intrigued, put down his cutlery and turned to Alex, ready to listen to him. "Tell me everything. I feel you have big news. "

Alex paused, savoring the moment before sharing his news. "My father retired from the current affairs of Karter Finance to enter politics. He thinks he can make a difference on a larger scale, and I agree with him. It's the right time for him. "

Lucas: "Richard in politics, it makes sense. What about you then? What does this mean for you?"

Alex: "That means I'm taking over as head of Karter Finance. It's an enormous challenge, but I feel ready. I can run the company in my way while respecting my father's legacy. "

Lucas, delighted for his friend, raised his glass: "It's amazing, Alex. That's what you're made for, I've always known that. To you, and to this new chapter!

They toasted after a while. Lucas spoke again, curious to know more.

"What about Tori in all this? She hasn't contacted me recently. "

Alex took a sip of his drink before answering, his tone remaining optimistic.

"There have been complications with Tori. She found herself involved in affairs that led to her being arrested. She will auction the property she inherited to pay for bail. It's unfortunate, but it's part of what needs managing. "

Lucas listened intently, absorbing the information. "It's a turning point for everyone, it seems. But I know you'll be able to navigate through it all. "

Alex smiles, reinforced by his friend's confidence. "Yes, this is a turning point, but I am ready to cope. Expert hands guide Karter Finance; I am determined to lead us forward. "

Lucas believes in your decision-making abilities, as always. "

Alex: "And you at the newspaper? "

Lucas: "You don't know the news! I got appointed, not my editorial manager."

Alex: "Well done Lucas! you will soon have exclusive titles about the Karter family"

Lunch continued in a light and hopeful atmosphere. The two friends exchanged laughter and memories, savoring every moment.

A few weeks pass ...

The Karter mansion, usually a place of calm and prestige, was today invaded by the typical effervescence of the preparations for an American election campaign. Inside, the once peaceful large rooms were now teeming with members of the campaign staff, each going about their tasks with overflowing energy. Richard's office, usually a sanctuary for quiet reflection, had turned into a real political headquarters.

Assistants strolled between the rooms, carrying stacks of documents, laptops, and phones, constantly on alert. The assistants set up meeting tables in several rooms, covering them with strategic maps, recent polls, and donor lists. On the walls, whiteboards displayed tight schedules, fundraising goals, and carefully chosen campaign slogans. Television screens continuously broadcast the news, analyzing each movement of the candidates.

Richard, amidst the chaos, conversed with his campaign manager, a sharply dressed man with intense eyes, holding a black notebook and diligently recording campaign details. Next to him, a young woman was furiously tapping on her laptop, adjusting messages for social networks and coordinating upcoming publications. A little further on, the press relations manager meticulously reviewed the key points of the planned interviews, checking each word carefully to ensure it would be interpreted in the desired way.

Margaret, playing her role to perfection, smiled and greeted each member of the staff who passed, while making sure that Richard had everything he needed. Although she was not directly involved in strategic decisions, her presence was a constant reminder of the image of the united and solid family that Richard wanted to project.

Alex, meanwhile, was watching the scene from a corner of the room, his arms folded. He was actively involved in discussions with Richard, offering ideas on how to reach key voters. "The southern district is essential," he said, pointing to a map of the city. "If we want to win this election, we need to focus our efforts there."

Richard nodded, his gaze fixed on the map. "We ensure each message is clear, and that our proposals respond to the concerns of voters."

The campaign team intervened, stressing the importance of public appearances. "We need to intensify the campaign events. No more field visits, no more speeches in local communities. You must present yourself as the man who takes action and creates change. "

Amidst the discussions, a figure silently entered the room like a gliding shadow. Unlike the other members of the family, she remained in retreat, observing everything with a calculating coldness. His eyes rested alternately on the members of the staff, on the whiteboards covered with strategies, and finally on his father, who, without knowing it, was the target of his dark thoughts.

Emma stayed away, like a feline watching the prey. No one really paid attention to her, used to seeing her as a silent spectator looking for loopholes to exploit.

"Richard" Margaret intervened with a smile, interrupting the discussion briefly to remind us of the importance of public image. "Don't forget that every word counts. You must sincerely commit to making the voters feel you are dedicated to them. "

Richard nodded, absorbed in the tasks at hand, while Alex added: "And we have to be ready to answer the hard questions. Transparency will be our asset. "

Richard nodded, absorbed in the tasks at hand, while Alex added: "And we have to be ready to answer the hard questions. Transparency will be our asset. "

The staff continued to be active around them, making calls, sending emails, and organizing the next steps of the campaign. The team felt the intensity of the preparations, understanding the moment's significance. Emma remained silent, her presence barely noticed, but her mind was in turmoil, ready to exploit every opportunity to serve her own purposes.

Richard Karter's supporters gathered in the city's central park, where the afternoon was sunny and teeming with life, to hear his speech. The platform, adorned with banners and slogans, dominated the stage, while flags fluttered in the wind, symbolizing the hope and ambition of a new era for the city. The crowd, dense and attentive, had their eyes riveted on the platform where Richard, accompanied by his family, was preparing to deliver a key speech for his election campaign.

Margaret, at her side, Alex, a little removed, was watching the scene with pride.

Richard stepped up to the microphone.

"My dear fellow citizens," he began in an assured voice, "we are at a crucial moment for the future of our city. Together, let us build a better future, a future where everyone finds their place and where we face the challenges with determination. "

The applause rang out, and Richard continued developing his plans for the city with a passion that captivated the audience.

But suddenly, a familiar figure stood out from the background. Emma, who had hitherto remained behind, advanced slowly towards the front of the platform. Richard's face revealed surprise as she walked over to the microphone. He looked at her, surprised by her unexpected words.

Margaret and Alex exchanged an alarmed look, concern mingling with disbelief. The crowd, meanwhile, had fallen silent, intrigued by this unexpected intervention.

Emma placed herself in front of the microphone, an enigmatic smile stretching her lips. Her eyes shone with a gleam of delight.

"Ladies and gentlemen," she began, her voice soft yet penetrating, immediately capturing attention.

"You know my father, a man of principles, a man whom we all admire. But today I want to tell you about a lesser-known aspect of politics. "

Richard felt his heart beat faster, the effect of surprise pinning him on the spot. He observed, mindful that a sudden reaction could heighten the tension of this unexpected moment.

"Politics, "Emma continued, her words carefully chosen, "is not simply a matter of promises and beautiful speeches. It involves complex decisions, choices that are sometimes difficult to understand for those who are not directly involved. Truths, let's say... uncomfortable, which we prefer to keep in silence so as not to disturb the fragile balances. "

The crowd listened intently; the murmurs rising softly as Emma's innuendo took shape.

Emma, feeling the effect of her words, stung one last time, adding a sharp implication :

"My father has always done his best for this city, but I sincerely hope that he will not neglect his commitments to you, as he may have done in the past... with his own daughter. "

A heavy silence fell over the crowd, the gravity of Emma's statement hitting the audience full force. Richard, bewildered, felt the ground slipping away from under him. The crowd held its breath, trying to grasp Emma's words and feeling the shock wave.

Richard stepped forward calmly. He gently placed a hand on Emma, offering both comfort and reassurance.

"Thank you, Emma, for these thoughts," he said with a controlled smile, taking the microphone.

In politics, like in life, we must always make hard decisions. But the integrity and love of this city guides every choice I make. I am committed to serving this community honestly and transparently."

The applause rang out again, but they were less enthusiastic, imbued with a slight doubt. Richard ended his speech by emphasizing his plans for the city, trying to dispel the shadow that Emma's words had cast.

Emma, meanwhile, stepped back gently, her subtle smile still clinging to her lips. She had sown doubt, just enough to shake without destroying. A well-placed blow in a power game that she had barely begun to play.

As Richard concluded his speech with new vigor, the crowd, although reassured. Emma left her mark, revealing a complex campaign against the surface.

Richard's speech still echoed in the air, but Alex's attention remained fixed on Emma. Near the cocktail buffet, a bottle of champagne in his hand, his gaze fixed on Richard's campaign cake. Alex knew he had to intervene before the situation got worse.

He quickly approached her. When he reached Emma, he found her uncorking the bottle, a defiant smile on her lips.

"Emma, what are you doing? "He asked

Emma looked up at him, a mischievous glint in her eyes.

"Me? I'm celebrating, "she replied with a false lightness, while popping the cork. The champagne gushes, and before Alex can react, she pours the sparkling liquid on the cake, destroying in an instant this carefully prepared symbol.

"Emma, stop! "Alex cried." He tried to grab the bottle, but Emma stepped back a step, laughing softly.

"Why should I stop, Alex? "She launched, her icy tone contrasting with her smirk." "Richard thinks he can buy everything, control everything... even his own daughter's silence. "

Alex, his eyes wide, felt the anger rising in him. "Do you truly believe this is the answer?" Destroy everything he built just to get back at you? "

Emma shrugged her shoulders, emptying the last drops of champagne on the cake.

"I want him to understand that everything he has built can collapse in an instant. He ignored me for too long, Alex. Now he will learn that I am not a secondary piece in his game. "

Alex took a step forward, his gaze hardening.

"It's not just a cake, Emma. It's the entire campaign that you're sabotaging. Is that really what you want?"

Emma stared him straight in the eyes, her smile fading to give way to an icy expression.

"I want him to know that I will no longer be silent. He can't buy my silence like he's bought so many other things. He is mistaken if he thinks everything can be sorted out with money or promises. "

She paused, letting her words soak in. Then, stepping slightly closer to Alex, she added in a lower voice, but just as sharp:

"I want to regain my place in this family, Alex. I want to do it now, no delay. If Richard refuses, or if someone tries to push me aside again, I will make sure that his political ambitions collapse as quickly as this cake. "

Alex paused, realizing the gravity of the situation.

"Are you serious?"

Emma, without another word, turned on her heels, leaving the empty bottle on the sideboard.

"Believe me, Alex, I'm very serious. And if our dear father wants to avoid a disaster, he knows what he has to do. "

As she walked away, Emma hadn't just destroyed a cake. She had issued an ultimatum showing her determination. He had to shoot, yet remained clueless about calming the storm, a threat to all.

After his speech, Richard, angry as ever, paced the office, his footsteps echoing heavily on the marble floor. His voice thundered, shaking the walls of the room.

"She dared, Alex! "roars Richard, his voice charged with rage. "My daughter, in my countryside! She ruined a supposed triumph with sabotage. "

Alex He knew his father was on the verge of an explosion, but he had to keep calm.

"We have to keep a cool head. Emma is playing a dangerous game, but we can still bring her to her senses. "

Richard turned to him, his gaze aflame.

"Bring her to her senses? Should I help her regain her senses after her recent actions? "He hit the desk with his fist, startling Alex. "She wants war, she will have it! "

Alex carefully searching for his words.

"You can't give her what she wants, father. She wants to see you lose control, to see you react impulsively. That's exactly what she's waiting for. "

"And what are you proposing, Alex? That I crash in front of her? That I let her trample on everything I've built? Richard stopped in front of his son, his eyes burning with fury. "I will not allow myself to be humiliated by my daughter! "

Alex: "No, but you can make it harmless. Does she desire a role in our family? Let's give her what she wants, but on our terms. "

Richard narrowed his eyes, suspicious. "What are you suggesting? "

"Appoint her campaign director," Alex replied.

Richard burst out laughing, a mirthless laugh. "Do you want to give her power after what she just did? This is crazy, Alex! "

Alex supported his father's gaze, not flinching.

"It's that, or let her continue to destroy you from the inside. Do you think she's going to stop there? She's ready for anything, and you know it. If we don't give her a bone to gnaw on, she's going to keep scratching until there's nothing left. "

Richard stepped back, shaking his head.

Is this truly the solution? Give her what she wants? "

"That's not what she wants," Alex replied, his eyes shining with determination. "That's what she thinks she wants. But by putting her at the center of your campaign, we're making her accountable. If she sabotages something again, she will no longer harm only you, but herself. "

Against the idea, but he saw the logic in his son's words. "It's risky, Alex. perilous. "

Each campaign day holds risk, Alex replied defiantly. "But it's a risk you have to take. Either you control her, or she destroys us all. "

Richard stared at his son, a gleam of admiration mixed with anger in his eyes.

"Very well," he said finally. "Make him this offer. She must grasp this as her last opportunity. If she refuses or betrays again, I won't be responsible anymore. "

Alex: "I'll talk to him. And I'll make sure she understands what's at stake. "

Richard turned on his heels, heading for the window.

"Let it be clear, Alex. If she accepts, she plays by our rules. Not hers. And if she plays a double game... "

Alex: "She won't. "

Richard: "Make sure she knows that. This family must remain united. I will not accept any other betrayal. "

Alex was prepared to confront Emma, clarifying that the time for games had ended.

The successful work of this political preparation led to agreements reached after weeks of nullified dialogues.

Karter mansion's room turned into an elegant press conference stage. Journalists from Greenwood Hills, including Lucas, representing the *Greenwood Hills Journal*, had gathered for the long-awaited announcement. Richard and Alex, ready to unveil a new campaign strategy, were in the spotlight. The tension was palpable, but they orchestrated everything to show an image of a united family, determined to conquer the political future of the city.

The cameras were in place, and the flashes were already crackling as Richard spoke, a confident smile on his lips. He began with a summary of his vision for Greenwood Hills, reinforcing his commitment to transforming the city into a place of prosperity for all.

"My dear friends, residents of Greenwood Hills," Richard said, addressing the press, "together as a community and as a family, we will overcome these obstacles that pave the road to the future with challenges." Today, I am very pleased to announce a strengthening of our campaign. "

He paused, his gaze turning to Emma, who was standing by his side, calm and inscrutable. "My daughter, Emma Karter, is going to join our team as campaign director. His determination and his sense of strategy will be valuable assets to carry out this mission. "

Whispers ran through the room, and the journalists frantically took notes. The expected announcement had a powerful impact, solidifying the image of a united family in tough times.

With a controlled smile on her lips, Emma stepped up to the microphone, her eyes defiant.

"Thank you for this opportunity," she began, her clear voice echoing in the room. I am honored and determined to ensure campaign success. "

Then, in a calculated movement, she turned her head slightly towards the crowd, and her smile widened.

"I would also like to thank my fiancee for her unwavering support. I know that, just like me, our family will well accept and respect her. "

A tense silence followed his words, and a murmur of astonishment passed through the assembly. Journalists exchanged surprised glances at the unexpected revelation. Lucas, who was there to cover the event, quickly noted the information, aware of the twist it represented.

Alex stood near Emma. This announcement, although half expected, carried with it a new complexity.

Richard, despite his apparent calmness, stiffened slightly. He knew that this statement would attract special attention, not only to Emma but also to their family. He stepped forward to the microphone again:

"As you can see, "Richard began, "it shows that our family has a great open-mindedness. As modern individuals, this campaign symbolizes modernity for our city. "

The applause rang out in the room. Emma had thrown a new stone into the water, creating waves that would spread far beyond this conference.

As the evening shadows enveloped the great hall of the Karter Mansion, symbol of the discreet opulence peculiar to Greenwood Hills, a heavy silence set in, barely masking the tensions that continued to shake this perfect family. The press conference had ended, but its repercussions went far beyond the present moment.

Richard stood by the wide bay window of his office, his gaze lost in the darkness that engulfed the vast lawns and the alleys lined with centuries-old oaks. The smile he had displayed in front of the cameras vanished, but determination shone in his eyes. What had started as a triumphal march to the Greenwood Hills Town Hall had turned into a real family battlefield. Still, Richard knew he couldn't flex. His strength was now to guide his family through the coming storms.

The following days breathed new life into the countryside. True to her ambition, Emma fully invests herself in her role as Campaign director, bringing renewed energy and bold ideas to the table. Every initiative, every decision testified to his desire for recognition and his desire to prove his worth. But behind her actions, a doubt remained: was Emma acting for her father's successor to serve her own ambitions? His impassive expression may have concealed more complex designs, leaving uncertainty hanging over the future of the Karter family.

Margaret watched her daughter-in-law's maneuvers with a mixture of concern and defiance. Their relationship, marked by latent tension, was a silent struggle for control and recognition within the family. Margaret, strong in her traditional role, saw Emma as a rival, while Emma sought to impose herself in a world where family power was the key to everything. This dynamic added a fragility to the already precarious balance of the Karter family, well known in the influential circles of Greenwood Hills.

For his part, Alex was trying to maintain the delicate balance between his father's ambitions and his sister's aspirations. Success of campaign relied on Karters presenting the united front, matching city's expectations.

Election day was approaching, bringing increasing pressure. Richard, facing the gathered crowd, felt the moment's gravity. Surrounded by his family, he was ready to do whatever was necessary to accomplish his mission.

However, he sought more than just a political triumph. It was a chance of redemption for his family, the opportunity to prove that, despite betrayals, doubts and conflicts, they could remain united. He wanted to project a modern, open-minded family image at the press conference, not just for the public but also for themselves.

Election night buzzed with anticipation, each ballot heavy, each glance tense. Finally, the news broke: The people elected Richard Karter as the mayor of Greenwood Hills. A resounding victory, marked however by the family hardships they had gone through.

In the following days, the city celebrated its new mayor, while the Karter family enjoyed a victory tinged with realism. Richard had achieved his goal, but he knew that the real victory lay elsewhere. She promised a renewed unity, a family that endured storms. The tense relationship between Margaret and Emma remained an unresolved battlefield, where each was still trying to mark its territory, under the eyes of a society attentive to the slightest missteps of the powerful.

The campaign's end marked Alex's new era of responsibility. With Richard now focused on his duties as mayor, the management of Karter Finance fell entirely on him. He accepted this role with intact determination, aware of the challenges ahead, but with a lesson learned: true strength lies in unity, and it is this unity that he would strive to preserve at all costs.

The Karter mansion, witness of conflicts and reconciliations, gradually regained its serenity. But he kept the echoes of past struggles, realized ambitions, and new promises. The Karter family, despite everything, was ready to face the future together, stronger than ever.

The Karters were starting a new chapter as the sun rose over Greenwood Hills. A page where a determined family embraces modernity, open-mindedness, and resilience, tracing their path in the city's history and their own.

About the Author: Olivia Coldwell

Olivia Coldwell is an American novelist renowned for her stories that blend striking realism, psychological tension, and suspense. Growing up in the elegant suburbs of New York State, she draws from the mysteries hidden behind impeccable facades to craft narratives filled with unexpected twists. Passionate about cinema, she brings a precise, cinematic approach to her novels, making her plots both visual and captivating. Her works explore the contradictions of modern life, offering surprises on every page that keep readers on the edge of their seats.